MW01048081

Also by the author

The Night Action
Man on Fire

STREET SMARTS

Bruce Reeves

BEAUFORT BOOKS, INC.
New York / Toronto

No character in this book is intended to
represent any actual person; all incidents are entirely fictional in nature.

Library of Congress Cataloging in Publication Data

Reeves, Bruce Douglas.
Street smarts.

SUMMARY: A teenage girl who has been reared in a
Berkeley commune and a battered and abused neighborhood
boy decide to run away to San Francisco although neither
is prepared for the dangers and temptations of street life.
[1. Runaways—Fiction] I. Title.
PZ7.R2558St 1981 [Fic] 80-28256
ISBN 0-8253-0047-9

Published in the United States by Beaufort Books, Inc.,
New York. Published simultaneously in Canada by
Nelson, Foster and Scott Ltd.
Printed in the U.S.A. First Edition
10 9 8 7 6 5 4 3 2 1

For Simone, my best critic

STREET SMARTS

1

T.C. sat on the wooden steps of the back porch, her eyes hot and moist, her cheek still inflamed, and asked herself over and over: Why? She hadn't done anything. Just made a joke. She always joked and made wisecracks. Why should he hit her because she made a joke?

Adults could say what they pleased and nobody got mad. But let *her* say one little thing to her father and she got it right across the cheek.

She wouldn't take that from him, or anybody else.

Still feeling sorry for herself, T.C. wandered into the storeroom. A scrawny kid stood there with an apple in one hand and a slice of dill pickle in the other. A red scar snaked from his forehead up into his hairline. He jumped back and growled at her, saliva and pickle juice dripping from the corners of his mouth.

For a minute, T.C. was scared, even if the kid was only eight or nine and no higher than her shoulder. She thought that he must be crazy, like a mad dog or one of those rabid squirrels she had read about in the newspaper, and was going to attack her. She had heard how awful a human bite could be, and from the look of him the bite of this filthy little boy would be worse than most.

But he didn't jump out of the corner he had backed into, or bite her leg, or try to tear out her throat with his broken teeth. He sat on the floor behind the boxes of flour and the barrel of apples and cried—at least, T.C. guessed it was crying. It wasn't like any crying she had ever heard before in her eleven, almost twelve years.

Tears ran down the boy's smudged, bruised face, and he rubbed his eyes and cheeks with both fists, exposing awful-looking sores on his skinny, bare arms, but the sound that came out of his mouth seemed to bubble up from deep in his throat.

How had he got here? He wasn't part of their family. He was an outsider and shouldn't have been in the house. But when she watched his big, wet eyes and heard his terrified, animal-like noises, she realized that this boy wasn't anybody to be either afraid of or mad at.

He was someone to feel sorry for. Maybe somebody to help. He looked like a stray, a lost animal. More than anything else, T.C. liked to pick up stray animals and care for them. She was proud and stubborn and liked to make wisecracks and could hold a grudge for days, but if a lost dog or cat needed love or care, she would forget about everything else. There was nothing that she wouldn't do to help a miserable little creature.

"It doesn't matter," she told the boy. "You can have the apple. The pickles, too. I won't tell."

He grunted at her, but didn't change his defensive posture.

T.C. had noticed the ugly little kid a few times around the neighborhood. He always looked as if he had just lost a fight. She had never seen him when his face and arms and any other visible part of his body weren't covered with bruises and scabs and running sores.

She had caught other boys making fun of him and had chased them away, but boys were savages. T.C. had never met a single boy who wasn't mean. As far as she could tell, most of them didn't change much when they grew up. Her own father, she had believed until today, was an exception, and, of course, Neil, but he was practically a saint, so he didn't count.

T.C. (her real name was Teresa Carlotta, but she hated it and made everyone call her T.C. on pain of death) finally persuaded the boy that she wasn't going to hurt him, and led him through the old-fashioned kitchen to the back porch. So many people constantly went in and out of the house that she couldn't be sure somebody hadn't already spotted him.

One of the disadvantages of this kind of household was the lack of privacy. Nobody else in the commune seemed to be bothered by it, but T.C. hated having so many people around all the time. It wasn't just that she hadn't had a room of her own since she was five years old. She felt as if she had grown up in an ant hill. It was impossible to have a real secret, one that she could be sure nobody else would discover.

Snot rolling down his upper lip, the boy stared at her and bit into the yellow apple still clutched in his fist.

He *was* awfully skinny, she realized. She wondered where he lived. Probably in one of those shabby houses, toward Oakland. But you couldn't tell: Sometimes the poorest people lived in neat houses and the folks with money didn't give a damn about taking care of their house or yard. Their place, hers, always looked good because they had strict rules about keeping it up. Everybody had to take a turn on yard duty each week. Making the yard look nice was as important as kitchen duty or housekeeping or anything else, because it affected how they all appeared to the rest of the world. At least, that was what Neil told them.

"Come on," she said, not certain whether or not the boy could understand her. She pulled him by his pale, bruised wrist, and he flinched, jerking away from her. The sores on his forearm looked like burns. Now that she could see him more closely, she could make out welts on his neck and the side of his face, and deep abrasions in his scalp and dried blood in his hair. Somebody had been beating up on him.

"Listen," she whispered. "Don't you get enough to eat at home? Maybe I can persuade Neil to let you eat her sometimes. Okay?"

He ducked his head toward one bony shoulder, but there was no indication on his thin, dirty features that the boy either heard or comprehended what she was saying. She was beginning to think he was retarded, like Jimmy Bannister's sister Eloise, who had followed him to school that time and went to the bathroom in the middle of the playground, with the whole sixth grade watching.

Before she could try again to talk to the boy, T.C. heard voices approaching from the yard. She glanced out the window. It was Neil and one of the older boys. She remembered now that they were going to spend the morning reshingling the porch roof.

The ladder crashed against the side of the porch. The boy stood like a deer alarmed while feeding in a meadow and then darted past her. She saw him jump off the side of the porch and run away, hunched over, as if he hoped that nobody would see him if he made himself small.

Neil's heavy boots clattered up the wide plank steps to the porch. "Who was your friend? Didn't mean to scare him off."

"That was the deaf and dumb kid," said Jack, coming up behind Neil's broad back. Jack turned to T.C. as he came up onto the porch. "Is he going to be your new stray?"

"*Is* he deaf and dumb?" she asked Jack.

"He can't talk, can he? That's what deaf and dumb means."

Jack made her mad. He thought he was so smart, especially now that he was starting at the university this fall.

"Maybe he doesn't want to talk." Why she was defending that ugly little kid? He was nothing to her.

"What was he doing here, T.C.?" asked Neil.

She shrugged her shoulders, staring into Neil's fluffy white beard to avoid looking into his face. "I guess he was hungry," she said, at last.

"He was stealing food, wasn't he?" asked Jack.

"He's so skinny," yelled T.C. "And he's sick and somebody's been beating up on him. Why can't we help him?"

A smile maneuvered beneath the cottony growth of Neil's beard. "He *is* a stray you've picked up, isn't he? Well, there are worse habits. We'd better try to find out about him. Maybe somebody at lunch will have an idea about what to do with him."

T.C. nodded and slipped into the house. Damn Neil! She didn't want everybody talking about that boy. Then he wouldn't be hers anymore. Once again, the commune was going to butt into her life.

Privacy! Secrets! The luxury of not having people swarming around all the time, finding out everything! How she craved it. Where could she go to have some privacy? There was bound to be somebody in the girls' bedroom, upstairs. She never went to the playroom anymore. It was always filled with squealing babies and battling little kids.

She walked down the long redwood-paneled hallway to the front of the house and peered into the big, rectangular parlor. Sada, hugely pregnant, and Malvina, Neil's wife, sat by the stone-fronted fireplace, working on their macramé projects.

In a fit of disgust, T.C. turned away and walked directly into her mother. Averting her face, she muttered an apology and tried to walk around her mother's solid figure.

"T.C.! I want to talk to you."

Here it comes, thought T.C. The great peacemaker at work again! She gestured toward the other end of the hall, as if she had urgent business waiting down there, but her mother took her hand and held it firmly. "Your father's sorry about hitting you."

"Then he can tell me himself."

"He's upset, T.C. You hurt him very much with that remark."

"I was joking, for cryin' out loud. Where's his sense of humor?"

All she had said was, "Those who can *do,* those who can't *teach*!" Why should that offend him so much?

"You don't realize it, T.C., but your father's been under a lot of pressure at the university."

"They're not going to fire him, are they?"

"They're warning him T.C. Telling him to keep up with his research because it reflects on the department if he falls behind in his publishing."

"But he's a good teacher! Everybody says so! His students all like him!"

"Teaching isn't enough. Not for a professor in a big university."

T.C. nodded. "So that's why he got so mad. He thought I was hitting him when he . . . "

" . . . When he was down. Yes, that's about it."

"I didn't mean to."

"I know. Maybe you should tell him."

T.C. broke away from her mother. "I can't!"

"Why not? It'll be best coming from you."

"I just can't!" T.C. ran down the hall to the bathroom, locked herself in, and sat on the edge of the old-fashioned claw-footed tub. At least nobody could follow her in there!

She couldn't apologize. She had never been able to admit that she was wrong. It would kill her to go up to her father and beg his pardon. It was expecting too much of her to think that she should do it. She had her pride, too!

T.C. could hardly remember the time before she and her parents had joined Neil's commune. She hadn't started grammar school yet when they moved to the first big house the commune had settled in, and this fall she was entering junior high. A lot of people had come and gone in the seven years, but four of the original five families had stuck it out together. Most of the serious troubles had come from folks who had joined later. For a while, the place had been full of people who started with loud-mouthed enthusiasm but who refused to work or follow Neil's rules. She guessed that Neil and his rules ("The Second Ten Commandments," her father called them) were the main reasons the commune had lasted so long.

What really made her mad was that nobody had ever asked her if *she* wanted to be part of any commune. She and the other kids had been dragged along. The grown-ups had paraded all kinds of reasons why it was supposed to be good for kids to grow up in a commune: other kids to play with, emotional security, learning to share, acquiring proper values, on and on. . . . She guessed that it had been all right when she was little. It was less lonely than being an only child. But when you got to be eleven or twelve, then you wanted to lead a normal life, with a mother and father and maybe a sister or brother, in a regular house, where you didn't have to worry about how your teachers or school friends would react when you told them that you were part of a "family" that included twenty-two adults and thirteen children. (Not to speak of dogs, cats, rabbits, chickens, and other pets.)

If anybody guessed about the commune, she pointed out that the members of her commune were not hippies. Her father was a professor at the university and Margaret was a librarian and Jeff was a high school French teacher and Neil wrote books and had had articles published in magazines like *Harper's* and *New West* and *California Living*. A big white beard and white hair that reached to his shoulders didn't make Neil a hippie. He looked more like old pictures of Moses than he did like any hippie she ever had seen.

The bathroom door rattled. "Hey, who's in there?"

It was Kevin, nasty thirteen-year-old Kevin, who thought he was such a hotshot because Neil bragged about Kevin's vegetable garden. Who cared about his vegetables? Anybody could grow a bunch of tomatoes and carrots and corn and stuff, if they were stupid enough to want to. T.C. ignored Kevin.

He pounded on the door a while and cursed and finally left. T.C. sat on the edge of the tub and made faces at the mirror.

Then somebody else was knocking on the bathroom door. This time it was an adult. She reached over and flushed the toilet and noisily washed her hands.

"Are you sick, dear?" asked Malvina, when T.C. finally came out of the bathroom.

"Only in my head!"

T.C. darted past the small white-haired woman. Sometimes, Malvina's goodness made T.C. want to throw up. She fled the house and, striding along the sidewalk, mentally listed her faults.

She was proud, to begin with, and vain. Not vain of her looks—they were nothing to brag about—but of her brains. She was smart and she was gifted with a number of talents (through no fault of her own, her father liked to remind her). Even if it was chance that she could draw passibly and sing better than average and had a way with putting words together, it was enjoyable possessing these talents, and often an advantage. Her temper was less of an advantage and impatient nature still less of one.

She stopped at Park and Shop and bought a couple of Milky Way candy bars. Then, as she headed past the city swimming pool, next to the junior high she would be attending, she saw that boy again.

Half-distracted by the squeals and shouts coming from the pool behind the wire and redwood slat fence, she stared across the street. Yes, it was him, and he looked as if he was crying.

Dodging a smoke-spewing bus, she ran over to him, and heard, as the roar of the bus faded, his peculiar half-animal, half-human sobbing.

He was hunkered down on the curb, his filthy face partially hidden behind his bony, scab-covered knees. Red welts blossomed on his arms and legs. They looked like burns, but she couldn't imagine that would have caused so many small circular burns over his body.

When she crouched beside him, he jumped up, at the same time raising an arm as if to ward off a blow. Then he seemed to recognize her and lowered his arm. He stared at her, his mouth dangling open, his bruised knuckles rubbing back and forth over his damp lips.

"Here," she said, thrusting one of her candy bars into his fist. "You like Milky Ways? They're my favorite."

His fingers closed around the candy bar and he glanced up and down the street, as if to see if there was anybody near who might take it away from him. Then he ripped open the paper and stuffed the chocolate-coated candy into his mouth.

T.C. felt a chill run through her. The way this kid gobbled the candy gave her the creeps. Something about him scared her, but she didn't know what or why.

"Come on," she said, nodding toward the playground across the street by the swimming pool.

But the boy looked at her, his eyes shifting suspiciously, and then, dropping the Milky Way wrapper at her feet, fled.

Darn him, anyway, she thought; why did he have to keep bugging her?

She didn't feel like eating her candy bar, now. She shoved it deep into her pocket and hiked on down the street.

What about that boy's parents? Why didn't they take care of him?

T.C. couldn't understand how any mother or father could let a child wander around in that condition. Maybe it was nobody's fault if he was deaf and dumb, but those rags he was wearing, and the sores all over his body! His hair was filthy and matted and there were yellowish crusts and cracks in the skin around his eyes and in the corners of his mouth. It was obvious that he didn't get enough to eat.

Some parents ought to be reported to the police, T.C. decided. They ought to be locked up and have the key thrown away.

But maybe he doesn't have a mother and father. Maybe he's an orphan. Or, he could be a runaway. Maybe he doesn't have a place to live. What if he's living in the park, or hiding out in an alley at night?

His parents could be divorced. Maybe he lives alone with his mother and she's away at work all day and doesn't know about how he's so sick and—no, that's stupid. Anybody who even looks at the kid can see what a miserable mess he is.

Either he's an orphan or a runaway or his parents ought to be in jail.

To T.C. something was either right or it was wrong. And the condition of that boy was definitely wrong. Parents! They were enough to drive you crazy. Her own mom and dad meant well, but she couldn't stand being around them. They didn't have much patience with her, either, these days.

Probably it was her own fault. Everybody else in the commune was perfect, and she was a selfish brat. She screamed and yelled and lost her temper and made wisecracks all over the place, and everybody was so *patient*! It made her want to puke. She was almost glad that her father had got mad at her and slapped her face. She hated living with a bunch of goody-goodies.

T.C. held that everyone should speak up for what he or she believed in. Her favorite motto was from the American Revolution: "Don't tread on me!" She had a picture of the flag with the coiled snake on it above her bed. The other girls thought it was creepy, but she didn't care. It showed how she felt.

Someday, she thought, it might be possible for them to be friends, her parents and herself. When she was grown up. But, right now, she was furious most of the time, and always in hot water.

Why, oh, why, couldn't she be a normal girl in a normal family, where the father went to the office every day and the mother stayed home and cleaned house and took care of the kids?

But she knew it was a dumb idea, and didn't pursue it any further.

She kicked at a bolt in the gutter. The rusty bolt rolled a couple of feet and stopped against a crushed beer can. And that was something else! Everywhere she turned, she was reminded of her peculiar family and weird life.

Her father hated automobiles. He refused to drive a car. He even rode a bicycle to the campus and to his classes, his books and briefcase wedged into a wire basket. As if that wasn't bad enough, his hobby was collecting parts of automobiles that he found in the street. When he rode around town on his bike, he kept his eyes open for nuts and bolts and gas caps and other pieces that fell off moving cars. He claimed that all automobiles were deliberately made by the manufacturer to fall apart over a period of time. "The built-in trash factor," he called it.

In a shed behind the big house, he had a wooden crate with nearly forty pounds of nuts and bolts that he had collected in the last year on the streets of Berkeley and Oakland. Two other wooden crates beneath an aluminum ladder hanging on rusty iron hooks on the shed wall held pieces of wheels, hood ornaments, fragments of grillwork, radiator pieces, chromium decorations, handles to doors and windows, buttons to work radios and heaters, windshield wipers, even brake pedals and gearshift levers. All of these he had discovered lying in the streets.

T.C. thought it was the dumbest hobby she had ever heard of. What was he going to *do* with all these things?

Her father claimed that he had strarted the collection without intending to, just dropping the objects he found into his pockets. At home, he had begun to toss the souvenirs of his walks and bicycle trips into a box. Gradually, as the collection grew, he began to philosophize about it.

"It's incredible," he told everyone he could drag into the shed to admire his collection, his hands sifting through the assorted nuts, bolts, brake shoes, shims, springs, gas caps, hubcaps, wrenches, and screwdrivers. "They keep falling into the streets."

"But, Daddy," T.C. asked him, "is that any reason to collect them?"

He shrugged his shoulders. "I don't pick up everything," he told her. "I'm selective."

He explained that he had quit collecting hubcaps, spark plugs, and wheel balance weights almost at the outset, because there were too many of them. He had become a connoisseur of abandoned automobile parts.

T.C. thought that he was crazy. Everything about her family and the way they lived was crazy. Sometimes, it made her want to sit down on the curb and cry.

I'm a terrible person, she scolded herself. I don't appreciate how lucky I am. Like Dad says, I didn't do anything to deserve being born in America with plenty to eat and warm clothes and all the rest. Why isn't that enough for me? Why can't I be satisfied? All I do is make wisecracks and lose my temper. Why can't I be nicer? I want to be nice!

Unconsciously, perhaps, T.C.'s eyes followed the edge of the curb, as if she were, like her father, seeking out some lost piece of machinery, or a dream, to retrieve. She scuffed her way to another corner, looked up, about to cross the street, and saw that boy again, half a block ahead, kneeling on the pavement.

"The third time is a charm," she said, aloud, quoting one of Malvina's many old sayings. Maybe the proverb didn't exactly apply, but it did seem in some way important, that her life should come into contact three times in one day with that sad, mysterious little kid.

2

T.C. prowled around until noon and then let her feet take her home. One problem with growing as fast as she was ("about time!" she told herself, when examining her naked body in the bathroom mirror) was that she was always hungry. Even when she was angry she had to swallow her pride and appear at meals, or she would starve. Between-meal snacks in the commune were limited to an occasional orange or apple and a homemade granola and raisin mixture that T.C. loathed. If she spent her allowance on candy her skin broke out in bumps and she didn't have money left for movies or books.

T.C.'s steps crackled through the yellow and brown leaves that had fallen from the maples and elms that rose so tall on each side of the street. She enjoyed walking past the big old houses in her neighborhood, many of them covered with weathered redwood shingles, some decorated with carved Victorian fantasies. She could imagine carriages driving up from the bay beneath the same trees to the wide front porches of the houses. Seventy-five or a hundred years was nothing in the history of the world, she realized, but when she thought that the people who had lived in these houses when they were new were probably all dead, it seemed awesomely long ago.

She paused outside the gate and looked up at the pair of top-heavy houses that the commune called home. The new shingles had that striped half-weathered, half-raw look. A covered bridge with a couple of windows like partially closed eyes connected the houses on the second floor level. The bigger house had an additional floor above that, in which the boys had their dormitory. Sometimes, they made the whole building shake with their rowdiness.

Except for the bridge and the sign over the gate ("Twin Elms"), the houses didn't *look* freaky. They were two of the best-kept houses in the neighborhood. Nowdays, few families were big enough to need such large homes, so many of these houses were divided into apartments or rented rooms to students, like the house across the street that always had cars parked on the front lawn.

With a sigh, T.C. pushed open the redwood gate and trudged up the walk to the house. A change, that was what she needed. A big change in her life.

She was looking forward to junior high, but that wasn't the kind of change she meant. That was superficial. She wanted a change that would extend from her heart out to the whole world! She didn't know how to express it, even to herself, except to say that she wanted to experience "real life." She felt trapped, as if she had been picked up by a giant and set down in an artificial world with no connection to how most people live. She wanted to find out things for herself. She was tired of being protected.

Suddenly, she heard a familiar bell tinkle behind her and turned and saw her father walking his bike through the gate.

Embarrassed, they stared across the yard at each other. He parked his bicycle beside the front steps, snatched his bookbag and a paperback from the wire basket and, before she could turn her back on him, caught up with her on the wide front porch.

"I'm sorry I hit you," he said, not quite looking her in the face. "You made me angry, but I shouldn't have hit you."

T.C. said nothing. Her father waited, then thrust his hand into his corduroy jacket pocket. He held aloft a hefty three-inch bolt so important-looking that whatever it fell off probably didn't work anymore.

"That," he said, "is a good one."

T.C. realized that he was trying to make peace, so she nodded. She felt like a mother demonstrating patience as her son displays his collection of dead toads. "Yes Daddy, that's great."

One of the little boys, his cowlick nodding like a yellow flower, met them at the door. They just had time to wash and get to the table. Neil believed in meals being served on time.

The worst part of these meals in the commune was Neil's notion that there should be uplifting conversation while people ate. T.C. hated having to pay attention to grown-up conversation. And, sooner or later, Neil or Melvina or one of the other adults would turn to her and demand: "What do *you* think about this, T.C.?" More often than not, the spotlight would fall on her just when she had been daydreaming and had no idea what anybody was talking about. It was like being in school, only worse, because she didn't even get graded.

She sat between her mother and father, opposite pain-in-the-neck Kevin, who was acting smart-alecky because those were his vegetables from his garden on the table.

Only about a dozen people gathered around the huge oak table for lunch. Most of the adults had jobs during the day and couldn't get home at noon. Some days even her dad couldn't leave the university in time to bicycle across town.

Malvina and T.C.'s mother had prepared the meal, with help from some of the girls. They were the only grown-ups who didn't have outside jobs. They took care of the houses and did the cooking. Everybody else, even the males, had to take turns helping. As Neil said, that's what a commune means: cooperation.

The commune was saving money to buy a farm in Oregon. They had their eyes on two hundred and fifty acres, where some day they might be able to be genuinely independent of the rest of society. At the last business meeting, Neil had said that they had almost enough money saved up for the down payment and the first year's expenses. Everybody had seemed excited by the news.

Except T.C. As usual, she reacted differently than the others. Now that she was going to junior high school, she didn't want to move out to the sticks. What would she do in the middle of two hundred and fifty acres in southern Oregon? She wasn't old and fed up with the city life, the way Neil and Malvina were.

"Nobody's safe in the cities anymore," Neil was always telling the others. "Murders, rapes, hit-and-runs, you name it: You take your life in your hands walking to the grocery store. It'll be good to get away from it all, out where the air is clean and folks are friendly instead of crazy."

Malvina leaned forward, agreeing with her husband. "Old Mrs. Gillis, two doors down, had her purse snatched last week. She said it was just a boy who took it, a tall, skinny kid. He came running up from behind her and jerked it right out of her hand. He bumped into her so hard that she spun around in a circle and fell against a mailbox. If that mailbox hadn't been there, she would've fallen onto the pavement and hurt herself. You know how brittle old folks' bones are—and she's just turned eighty. Poor thing was so upset. She had all the money from cashing her Social Security check in her purse."

"We'll have to help her," said Neil. "We'll take a collection to make up the money she lost."

The conversation lingered briefly on the subject of city life, and then moved on to other subjects. T.C. was so busy thinking about how bored she would be stuck on a farm miles from civilization that she didn't realize that Neil was talking to her.

"I was saying, T.C., that you had an adventure today."

She looked at him blankly. She had no idea what he was talking about.

"This morning—when you found that boy in the storeroom?"

"Oh," she nodded.

Neil continued, to the others at the table: "Some of you may have noticed the boy around the neighborhood. He's small and dark and seems to have a skin problem."

"You mean that retarded kid?" asked Kevin, his mouth full of half-chewed carrot.

If anybody else had called the boy retarded, T.C. would have let it pass, but she wasn't going to let Kevin get away with it.

"He's *not* retarded!" she said. "He just needs help."

"What kind of help?" asked Malvina, as she passed the platter of cold cuts around the table.

"I don't know. But I saw him again, later, and he didn't look retarded to me. He was scared, but no wonder, if he's deaf and dumb and everybody picks on him all the time!"

"You gonna bring him home and keep him in a box under your bed?" asked Kevin. "Like you did with all those puppies and kittens and that rat?"

"It wasn't a rat, it was a guinea pig, and maybe I *will* bring him home and take care of him. Maybe I'll adopt him."

"You can't adopt a kid, stupid. You're too young." Kevin grinned triumphantly at T.C. She knew that her remark had been foolish, and it made her all the madder.

"Oh, go stick a carrot in your ear!" T.C. jumped up and ran from the table. She fled to the only place she could think of to be alone, the downstairs bathroom.

When she had the lock clicked into place, she sank to the cold tile floor and pressed her cheek against the side of the high, old-fashioned bathtub. She half-expected to hear footsteps outside the door and then either her mother's or her father's voice, but nobody came and she guessed that they had decided to leave her alone. Of course, now she would go without the rest of her lunch. And she was still hungry!

She remembered the candy bar in her sweater pocket, pulled it out and unwrapped it. Some lunch!

Later, when she felt certain that nobody was lurking in the hall, she unlocked the door and crept past the dining room. She heard Neil and her father discussing the move to Oregon. The way they were talking, it sounded definite.

T.C. hurried down the long hall, out the front door, and then ran to the gate. She was halfway down the block before she stopped running.

Why was she always so angry? Why did she make trouble all the time? Why was she at odds with everybody? Common sense told her that she couldn't always be right and they couldn't always be wrong, yet that was how it seemed to her. The more other people said she was wrong, the more she felt that she was right.

Her father had told her that people like would her more if she learned to hide her feelings. "Smile," he told her, "even when you don't feel like it, and you'll be surprised at the change it'll make in your life."

She wanted what she would never have as a kid: the freedom to live her own life. She wanted to live *real* life, not this fake existence in the commune.

"Don't be in such a rush to grow up," her mother told her. "You're not even twelve yet. Enjoy yourself, while you can."

That made T.C. want to laugh: Who said being a kid was so much fun? She couldn't wait to grow up. An adult can live by herself, where nobody can snoop, and can be her own boss. As far as T.C could figure, childhood was something to get through as quickly as possible.

As she hiked along the pavement, her ears picking up fragments of songs from student rooming houses and car radios, she wondered what the truth was about that deaf and dumb kid. After everything that had happened today, she wanted to find out about him. One thing she was sure of: Whatever she learned about the boy she would never tell anybody else.

T.C. didn't know why she was walking toward the university. It was just someplace to go. Often she took her skateboard or rollerskates to sail down the hills of the campus, but she had left the house in such a temper that she had forgotten them. She didn't even have her Frisbee with her. (Not her Frisbee, actually, but the one she shared with the other kids in the commune—the same with the skateboard. Only the rollerskates were really hers.)

Avoiding the crowds of Telegraph Avenue, she hiked

into the campus near the campanile. If she had a dime left, she could take the elevator to the top of the tower. The old man who ran the elevator might even let her ride for free. He liked kids. But the day was so smoggy, she decided to save the campanile for another time, when she would be able to gaze out over the bay to the Golden Gate and imagine herself sailing under the bridge on a steamship, maybe a freighter destined to stop at places like Hong Kong and Tokyo and Honolulu.

A Grayline tour bus chugged past, cameras and faces glued to its tinted windows, and she thought how funny it seemed that tourists paid money to take trips around Berkeley and the campus, and she had grown up here and didn't think that the place was anything special.

Except the bay. She loved the bay. And the sea gulls and pigeons and the little black mud hens and occasional pelicans that you saw hopping around on the mudflats during the low tide. Now people were lousing up the bay, too, filling it with garbage and polluting it with their oil spills. Killing the birds. It made her sick.

Stopping at the plaza by the student union, T.C. realized why she had come to the campus. She wanted to see her friend, the Orange Man. The Orange Man was another person folks thought was crazy, but he was no more crazy than anybody else. He spoke up for what he believed in, that was all. He never caused any trouble. And isn't it better to believe in oranges than in bombs?

T.C. made her way through the crowds in the big plaza between the glass-walled student union and the gray administration building, with its rows of columns like a Greek temple. She edged around the small cluster of disbelieving listeners in front of the Moon Man. The Moon Man wore a silver costume and helmet like somebody out of a cheap science fiction movie and sold property on the moon. For two dollars you could buy a fancy, printed "deed" to your own lunar estate.

Then she saw the Orange Man. He really was orange. Tall and skinny, with a halo of fuzzy orange hair, he wore an orange sweat shirt, orange trousers, and orange tennis shoes. He carried a gunnysack from which he plucked oranges to pass out to people as they walked by. Often people refused the gift, but he smiled and wished them well.

The Orange Man believed that every human being should eat at least two dozen oranges a day. Oranges, he preached, could make you immortal.

T.C. and the Orange Man were good freinds.

Vague, luminous, smiling, his gaunt face bobbing up and down, the orange-haired young man offered with gentle grace his beloved fruit. T.C. watched him from a few yards away, her heart filled with tenderness toward his trusting nature. All he wanted to do was help people. Yet so often they laughed at him, or worse. She felt an urge to run up and hug and protect him.

She jogged over and stared up at his face as if he were a tree growing from the concrete and shedding its fruit. He looked down, an orange in his palm ready to drop into her hand. A grin spread beneath his pointed nose as he recognized her.

"Hi there, T.C. Have an orange."

"Thank you." Solemnly, she accepted his offering, balancing it in her hand as if it were something rich and strange. Then they looked at each other for a few minutes. They didn't say anything; they just looked.

Finally, she spoke: "I don't know what to do."

He nodded, as if he understood what she meant.

"They're giving you a bad time again." It was a statement, not a question.

"It's my own fault," she volunteered.

He shook his head. "Nobody's fault," he replied. "But you have to do what you have to do. Look at me. I have to give people oranges. Whatever happens, that's what I have to do."

"And me?" asked T.C. eagerly. "What do I have to do?"

"You have to do what you have to do. You'll know when the time comes. And I'll tell you a secret. He bent over, until his mouth was close to her ear, his fuzzy orange head meeting her stringy brown hair. He smelled of oranges. "They won't be able to stop you."

He pulled his tall, skinny body upright again and gave her a significant look from the corners of his eyes. There seemed to be something so shrewd, so wise, in his pronouncement that she believed it completely.

"Don't be afraid," he told her, beginning to walk away, his bag of oranges slung over his shoulder. "And remember: Eat your oranges!"

Her eyes filling with tears, T.C. nodded.

She watched the Orange Man shuffle through the crowd, offering his gift of sunshine to the passersby. Then she ran in the opposite direction, between two ugly new classroom buildings, to the narrow, tree-sheltered creek that cut through the campus.

She threw herself on the damp grass beside the creek, beneath a small willow tree, and buried her face in her arms. She wasn't crying. But she *was* blocking out the world, even if only for a few minutes. Heedless of grass stains on her clothes, she pressed herself against the sloping lawn and lay so motionless that she thought she felt the revolving of the earth. She knew that the Orange Man was right: They would not be able to stop her.

At next Friday's business meeting it was decided that the commune would make the down payment on the two hundred and fifty acres in Oregon and move up to the farm in the spring. Neil and a couple of other members elected by the meeting would drive up to Oregon to make the arrangements. Everybody seemed enthusiastic about the prospect.

T.C. left the meeting early. One year of junior high and then she would have to move. It would be better for her not to start junior high here than to begin and then move. But she was just one unheard voice among all of the others. Since it didn't matter what she thought, there was no reason for her to remain at the meeting.

Besides, she had another problem to occupy her thoughts. T.C. had discovered where the boy lived. During the last few days, T.C. had busied herself with some detective work. What she had discovered had opened her eyes to a new and ugly world that she hadn't known existed.

She had prowled around the neighborhood until she had seen the boy again and then had followed him. He lived with a man and woman in a rundown duplex a couple of blocks away.

T.C. hid behind a car parked on the street. The boy didn't go into his house, but crouched in the dirt by the low step, as if waiting for something. A ramp made of worn planks led from the walk to the door, covering most of the step. The screen door opened and a thin, angry woman in a shapeless dress came out. She saw the boy and reached down and pulled him up by his hair, lifting his feet off the ground. "Didn't I tell you not to go out?" With her other hand she walloped him across the face, again and again.

The boy didn't cry or scream. He dangled like a rag doll from the woman's hand while she hit him.

"I know you can hear me!" she said. "So don't pretend you can't!" She dragged him into the house, slamming the door after her.

T.C. was too shocked to move. She had never seen a parent do anything like that to a child. She had watched a mother or father swat a kid on the backside to teach it not to run into the street, and her own father had slapped her that once, because of her big mouth, but this woman seemed to get a special satisfaction out of hitting the boy.

T.C. crept across the pavement and the dusty patch of earth and weeds to the curtainless, streaked window of the duplex apartment. From behind a brown and yellow shrub, she peered into the room. Beyond the dirty glass, she saw the woman and a man in a wheelchair. The man wore only faded blue jeans, covering bony, withered legs. His arms and upper torso were hugely muscled, as if to compensate for the puniness of his lower limbs. He was puffing on a cigarette. Both the man and woman gestured angrily as they talked. Then the boy crawled into view. The man reached over and hit the boy on the back with his fist. Then he pressed the lighted end of the cigarette on the boy's forearm. When the boy jumped, the man laughed.

T.C. sat back on the ground, her whole body trembling. What kind of people were they?

She wanted to see more, but was afraid to look. What should she do? Should she go to the police? Go home and tell her parents and Neil? Go next door and get one of the neighbors to stop those two from hurting the boy?

Would an adult believe her? And what reason could she give for snooping?

But the boy! What could she do about the boy?

She started to run home, stopped at the corner, then looked back, as if she expected her gaze to penetrate through the walls of the other houses so that she could see what was happening to the boy now. She turned toward home, again hesitated, her hands bunched into fists, and swore. Never in her eleven years had she felt so frustrated, so helpless. She wanted to smash things, to hurt somebody, to do something. But she was only a kid, and kids are powerless.

At this moment, she not only hated that man and woman in the duplex, but all grownups. It was as if all adults were conspiring to torment and hold down all children. In her mind, she was suffering the blows and burns inflicted on that skinny kid.

"Damn them!" she decided, "I'm not going to let them get away with it. I'm not!"

She ran back to the little one-story house with the two identical front doors behind identical low steps (except for the ramp) at the end of identical cracked concrete paths. She crunched through the weeds to the window and, cupping her hands around her eyes, peered into the front room.

The boy lay on the linoleum-covered floor, curled up like a wounded animal, hugging himself and twitching, as if with spasms of pain. The man, now wearing an open, short-sleeved shirt patterned with gaudy flowers and palm trees, wheeled in from another room. He started to guide his wheelchair past the boy and then, as if with an afterthought, paused and smacked the boy on the head with his powerful hand. Then he snatched up from a low table an already open can of beer.

Wiping drops of beer from his lips with the back of his hairy fist, the man stared at the window. T.C. dropped down below the sill and crawled away. Her hand mashed in some dog excrement, and she made a face and tried to wipe off the mess in the weeds.

While she stood in front of the house next door, rubbing her hand with an old Kleenex tissue that she found in her pocket, a green sedan drove up to the curb and a middle-aged man got out and carried a paper bag up the flagstone walk to the two-story house.

T.C. stepped in front of him. "Mister!" she cried out. "I need help!"

The bald-headed, stout man looked at her dubiously. A frown lowered his double chins.

"Those people in that house . . ." She pointed to the window through which she had watched the boy and the man and the woman. "They're doing awful things to that kid in there. I *saw* them. They kicked him and hit him and . . . and burned him on purpose with a cigarette."

The fat man looked angry for being bothered. "I can't do nothing about that. It ain't my business. He ain't my brat. He belongs to them."

He tried to walk around T.C., but she wouldn't let him get past her. "You mean they're his *parents*?"

"That's his mother, all right. He's the boy's stepfather. I can't go interfering with them punishing their own kid. Maybe he did something to deserve it. How do *I* know?"

The fat man clutched his bulgy paper sack firmly and marched around T.C. "Ain't none of my business," she heard him say, before he slammed the door of his house between them.

"But—wait!"

She couldn't believe that the man really didn't care. Was he right? Could people do whatever they wanted to their children? What about laws? Weren't there laws about things like that?

Slowly, T.C. walked to her own block. She still saw the

woman holding her son by the hair and hitting him with her hand, and that man in the wheelchair pressing the lighted cigarette onto the boy's skinny arm and then laughing as if it were a joke. She remembered every detail, but didn't know what to do about it.

Would all grown-ups be as indifferent as that neighbor? T.C. wanted to tell her father or Neil about what she had seen, but she was still mad at her parents and Neil and didn't want to involve them in her life any more than they were already. She was no baby, running to them every time she was in trouble. Besides, they wouldn't believe her. They'd smile and say that she was letting her imagination work overtime.

She saw two of the girls she knew from school walking up the block toward her. It was too late for her to dodge them. Sarah Louise was waving. Tanya leaned over and whispered something to Sarah Louise and they both laughed.

"Hi, T.C.!" said Sarah Louise.

"Hi!" said Tanya.

"Hi."

"What're you doing, T.C.?"

Could she tell them about her discovery? Ha. They were incapable of taking anything except boys seriously. They were only twelve, but already they were gushing over John Travolta and boys at school. They thought she acted superior, because she didn't care if boys noticed her. Sarah Louise and Tanya couldn't imagine anybody who didn't think the same way they did. They thought T.C. was peculiar, anyway, because she lived in a commune. They laughed at her because she used big words and liked to read and enjoyed homework, but they were a little afraid of her, too, because of her quick tongue and sarcastic wit.

T.C.'s one good friend had moved away this summer.

For years, T.C. and Norah had looked forward to entering junior high together, and then Norah's parents, who taught at the university, had gone to Africa to study grasshoppers, and now Norah was in Nairobi. Life, T.C. decided, was not fair.

"Why do you look so peculiar, T.C.? You got a secret, or something?"

T.C. shrugged her shoulders. "I just got a love letter from John Travolta, that's all."

"Okay, don't tell us." Tanya twisted her features into a haughty expression. "See if we care! You're not so hot, T.C. You'll find out when you get into junior high and don't have any friends. You're going to need us, because we know lots of the kids there, and you're going to come sucking up to us wanting to be friends and we won't pay any attention to you!"

The two girls sashayed down the street, leaving T.C. fuming on the sidewalk.

She almost wished that she had told them about that boy. It would've done them good to know what life was like for other people who had things to think about besides being popular. But she knew that it would have been futile. They wouldn't have understood. Their brains were too small.

All the same, T.C. wished that Norah were back. She needed a close friend, somebody she could confide in. Somebody to give her advice.

At home, she ran into her father before she could go upstairs. "I guess I'll have to get rid of my collection," he said. "I can't take it to Oregon. Maybe I'll sell it for scrap metal." He grinned and gestured with the book in his hand, forefinger marking his place. "All those nuts and bolts! I'll never find out how many a car could lose before falling apart."

T.C. opened her mouth to tell him about the boy, but he continued with his own thoughts.

"Did I ever tell you that I find the most nuts and bolts at intersections, T.C.? Bolts outnumber nuts three to one." He chuckled: "I love the idea of some car stopping for a red light someday and suddenly losing its fenders and doors and wheels, everything. Just collapsing in the middle of the street, like an old-time movie. Wouldn't that be funny?"

T.C. nodded and walked past her father. He was still talking as she climbed the stairs to the second floor.

"Don't be late for dinner," he called after her.

For a reply, he heard a door closing upstairs.

The bedroom was empty. T.C. stood in the center of the long room, turning around and around, as if she were looking for something. Her hands gestured in the vacant space.

I'm not afraid, she told herself. I can do things. I'm not a baby. I'll show them—all of them.

And herself: she'd show herself, too.

That night, it was T.C.'s turn to help with the dinner dishes. Her partner was Kevin, but even he couldn't get a rise out of her. His attempts at jokes got nowhere, and he finally gave up when she didn't come back at him with a single wisecrack or insult. Needling her was no fun if she didn't fight back.

As soon as the last dish was put away, T.C. fled the kitchen. She decided to fetch her sweater and go for a walk. She couldn't stand being trapped in that giant ant nest for another minute.

Upstairs, the little kids were screaming and bouncing, thumping on the floor, making the old house creak and groan like a ship in a storm. An old Beatles album was playing on the parlor stereo, and the thump-thump of a basketball could be heard, as eighteen-year-old Jack and one of the other boys took turns shooting for baskets.

T.C. stopped at the door of the TV room and glanced in. Half a dozen grown-ups sat staring at the old black and white set. It was only the evening news roundup. She had already turned her back on the television set when the words of one of the reporters caught her attention.

"How many youngsters in America are suffering the pain of child abuse?" T.C. leaned against the door frame and blinked at the television screen. "Nobody can say for certain, because of all crimes this is one of the least frequently reported, but it is safe to assume that in California alone thousands of boys and girls are mistreated every year."

The voice of the glossy-haired, mustached television reporter throbbed with professional compassion. Photographs of bruised, unhappy children flashed in quick succession on the screen as the announcer concluded his special, "in-depth" three-minute report.

T.C. didn't learn much from the man's rather general remarks, but for the first time she realized that it was not uncommon for adults, even parents, to beat up on kids.

"It's because kids aren't big enough to fight back. Grown-ups are cowards!" She hadn't meant to speak out loud, but everybody in the room turned and looked at her. Her face burning, she ran upstairs.

T.C. sat on her bed, beneath the poster of the "Don't Tread on Me!" flag, and thought about what she had just heard.

More and more, she resented the fact that children must depend upon adults for food and shelter. That was why adults could get away with shoving kids around the way they did. Look at the kids in the commune: Who asked them if they wanted to be part of it? But they had to go along with their parents' decisions, because their parents owned them. Wasn't that what that fat man had said? Kids are pets, like dogs or cats or white mice, and people can do what they please with their pets. Even kill them.

Sure, the kids in the commune were lucky. Nobody beat up on them. They ate well enough and had clothes and all that stuff. But they weren't free.

T.C. tied her sweater by the sleeves over her shoulders and ran down the back stairs and out the rear door. She passed the basketball players and ran around the house, under the second-floor bridge, to the front gate. There, peeking between the slates of the redwood fence, was the boy.

He looked up at her.

One part of T.C. wished that she had never set eyes on the kid; another part wanted to grab him and hug him until he squeaked. "Wait a minute!" she said.

She gestured for him to stay right where he was and then ran into the house. She tiptoed past the parlor and TV room and slipped into the kitchen. Nobody was there, although recently washed dishes were waiting to be put away. She filled a waxed paper sandwich bag with cookies and hid it beneath her sweater, which she carried over her arm.

The television and stereo made enough noise to cover her retreat, although she stumbled on the hall rug. In a minute, she was out by the front gate.

She gestured for the boy to follow her, and they set off down the street together. When they got away from the house, she gave him the sandwich bag of cookies.

His stubby, filthy hands ripped open the bag and began

stuffing the chocolate chip cookies into the red O of his mouth.

T.C. watched him with horrified fascination. This wasn't greed. It was more like starvation.

She felt in her pocket for the remains of her spending money, counted it, and decided to take him to Telegraph Avenue for a hot dog.

He finished the cookies, turned the bag inside out and licked it, and then ran his tongue over his fingers. All the while, he trotted along beside her like a puppy, staring up at her with his large, dark eyes.

Actually, he didn't look as bad as he had the last time T.C. had seen him. His jeans were ragged and dirty, but he wore a respectable if faded blue T-shirt over them. She didn't know what sores and wounds might be hidden by the shirt, but she didn't want to know, either.

A spasm of rage shook T.C. as she watched the scrawny little kid bouncing along beside her. If only she were big enough to give the boy's stepfather what he deserved. She visualized herself beating him up, just like John Wayne. And that would be just the beginning.

The boy kept up with her until they reached the crowds of Telegraph Avenue. Then he drew back and would have run away, but she held him firmly by his sticky hand. Dodging the evening shoppers, the sidewalk vendors, and the university students from the nearby dorms, she led him past the shops and restaurants, avoiding the corner where she knew the commune's stand would be set up with its array of macramé gifts and pots and candles. September on Telegraph Avenue always seemed like a carnival, as the area around the campus burst into activity after the summer lull.

T.C. hesitated by a long-haired golden retriever waiting

for its owner in front of a discount record store. She stroked its damp nose. It rolled its dumb-looking eyes and licked her hand, but when she tried to get the boy to pet the animal, he backed away, shaking his head.

Pushing her money across the linoleum-topped counter of the hot dog stand, T.C. looked down and saw the boy trembling with anticipation. When he wrapped his two hands around the huge hot dog she offered him, he risked a grin. T.C. realized that this was the first time she had seen the boy smile.

Mustard dribbling down his chin, bits of frankfurter and crumbs hanging from his thin lips, the boy kept pace with T.C. as she walked back up Telegraph Avenue. His cheeks bulged until he looked like a chipmunk. She paused to study store windows and give him a chance to concentrate on eating. When he finished, he licked his fingers, one by one.

She had half-decided to walk him home, but when they reached the corner of his street he ran off in a different direction.

It took two days after she saw the television report about abused children before T.C. accumulated nerve to ask her father what happened to people who beat up their kids.

"If it can be proven, their children are taken away from them. Sometimes the parents are put in jail. It's against the law to do things like that." Her father put his hand on her shoulder: "Why? Are you afraid I'm going to start beating you up?"

"No." But she didn't want to leave the subject there. "What about the kids? What happens to them? I mean, if the parents are arrested?"

"If they don't have somebody else to stay with, a relative

or somebody, I guess they're taken to a city or county home."

"Like an orphanage?"

"Yeah, something like that. They might be put in foster homes."

"What's that?"

"Folks who are paid to look after homeless kids. They take the kids into their own house."

"That would be okay, wouldn't it?"

"It depends. Some people who do it might be nice. Others might do it just for the money."

T.C. nodded. She understood.

"Why all the questions?"

"No reason. I just wondered."

She didn't feel like trying to make up an excuse. Let him think what he wanted. He'd forget it pretty soon. She knew from experience that adults don't take children seriously enough to worry very long about what concerns them. Most grown-ups aren't even curious about what goes through kids' heads.

Right now, T.C. wished that somebody would guess what was bothering her and take the responsibility away from her. She felt that she should do something, but she was afraid. Even if she told somebody, how did she know that the boy would be any better off? It would depend on what the grown-ups decided to do with him. She didn't like the idea of turning him over to strangers.

Late that night, after most of the household was in bed, T.C. waylaid Neil in the upstairs hallway. In his flowing caftan, white beard spread over his huge chest, he looked more than ever like an Old Testament prophet.

"Shouldn't you be in bed?"

"I was, but I couldn't sleep. I need to talk to you."

"Can't it wait until morning?"

"No." It had taken her long enough to work up her courage to talk to Neil, and she wasn't going to let him put her off.

"Okay, what is it?"

"It's about that boy, the one who acts like he's deaf and dumb." Neil nodded. "I found out where he lives and . . . other things about him."

Slowly, after several false starts, T.C. described what she had witnessed through the duplex windows, as well as how the boy was being starved. "If that isn't child abuse, what *is* it?" Neil didn't comment. He looked down at T.C., waiting to find out what she would say next.

"So I want to know, can we keep the boy? He likes me—I think he likes all of us, really. He's just shy. Can't we adopt him, or something? The police would be on our side. If they knew what his mother and stepfather are doing to him, I'll bet they'd put those two in jail!"

"T.C., the situation isn't as simple as that."

"What do you mean?" In the dim light of the hallway, T.C. strained to see Neil's face. "He wouldn't be any trouble. I'd take care of him. I promise."

"That's not what I mean."

"What is it, then? *Why* can't we adopt him?"

"He has a mother and stepfather already."

"But they torture him and starve him. I saw it."

"Yes, but physical child abuse—even the extreme kind—is hard to prove in court, T.C. It might be your word against theirs."

"And I'm only a kid!" Neil nodded. "Couldn't a doctor look at him and tell what they did to him?"

"Maybe, but it might be a very unpleasant business, T.C. I don't know if it would be wise at this time for the commune to get involved in a family dispute."

"It's *not* a family dispute! It's child abuse! They're torturing him! Neil, please help him!"

"Not so loud, T.C. People are sleeping in this house." He sent a smile through his whiskers and down over the great bulk that was his chest and belly until it crashed against her stubbornness. "I'll try to think if there's anything we can do—without getting directly involved—to help the boy."

"So you won't let the commune adopt him?"

Neil shook his head. "I don't see how we can. It's late, T.C. Better get into bed."

T.C. turned and padded down the hall to the bedroom she shared with the other girls. She should have known better, she told herself. Neil didn't care about anything but his stinky old commune.

She climbed onto her bed and sat with her arms folded, staring at the wall. Suddenly she reached up and tore down the poster of the coiled snake and the words "Don't Tread on Me!" What was the use?

They could walk over her any time they wanted.

3

Adults, she thought, staring at her reflection in the mirror, while she hacked at her hair with the scissors, adults are the cause of all the troubles in the world. *I'm* going to be different when *I* grow up. I'm not going to be like the rest.

Her upper teeth biting her lower lip, her body twisted from the waist, T.C. finished cutting on one side of her head and then lowered the scissors. Stepping back, she looked at the results. Pretty grim.

Relentlessly, she attacked the other side. Getting it even was the hard part. The hair got shorter and shorter until she looked like that actress who played Peter Pan on television. She fluffed it up with her hand and stepped away from the mirror.

"One, two, three," she counted, as slowly as she could, "four, five, six, seven, eight, nine, ten." She jumped back in front of the mirror, hoping that caught off guard she might like what she had done to herself.

"I don't care," she told her reflection. "I never *could* keep it nice, and it'll be easier to take care of now."

The handle on the door rattled. "Just a minute!"

"You again?" It was Kevin, "T.C., what do you do, live in there?"

"Go jump in the bay!"

She gathered up the cut locks and flushed them down the toilet, wrapped a towel around her head, as if she had just washed her hair, and unlocked the door. She almost collided with Kevin.

"Trying to make yourself beautiful? Give up, it's a losing battle."

T.C. did not condescend to make a reply. She ran to the bedroom she shared with Susan, Tina, and five-year-old Wendy. Only Wendy was there, playing with paper dolls on her bed. T.C. pulled the towel off her head and again examined her haircut.

It didn't look too bad. Maybe it would give her a kind of distinction: having short hair when everybody else wore it long. Her parents would hate it, but they had driven her to it. Neil and her parents, *all* of them, had pushed her too far, until she had had to do something crazy. Something to show them who she was. Now it was done, and she would have to face them. She stomped out of the bedroom, leaving five-year-old Wendy staring after her.

The sensation that she expected and hoped for when she appeared at dinner didn't occur. Kevin rolled his eyes, Susan and Tina whispered at her ("Oh, T.C., why'd you do it?"), Jack groaned, and her mother said, "Your *hair*!", making it sound as if she had lopped off an arm or a leg, but the others ignored T.C. and her haircut. They were too busy discussing Oregon and the future of the commune to be concerned with anything as trivial as T.C.'s hair.

I could cut my nose off, she thought, and nobody would give a damn.

After dinner, it was T.C.'s turn to help clear the table. As she did it, she managed to squirrel away a French bread roll, a hunk of cheese, and an apple for the boy. Every evening, she found him waiting for her near the gate. If anybody else approached he vanished, but he always returned.

T.C. didn't believe that the boy was either deaf or retarded. She thought that she had discovered real intelligence behind his eyes, and he seemed to understand her when she spoke to him. But either he couldn't or he wouldn't talk. When she asked him his name he stared past her, drooling slightly, or fidgeted with his ill-fitting, dirty clothes. She had tried to trick him into talking, sneaking up on him and suddenly shouting out a question or abruptly turning around and confronting him, but he never uttered a sound that was anything like a word. His garbled noises sounded like a speeded phonograph record. She listened to the weird jumble of sounds, trying vainly to pick out words, or even syllables. He didn't trust her enough yet, she decided, to let her hear him utter real words—genuine pieces of himself—but he would someday.

Even if she never heard his voice, he meant more to her than anybody else. Sure, she loved her mother and father and was fond of little Wendy and Malvina and most of the others in the commune. She even liked stupid Jack and obnoxious Kevin. But this kid, in scarcely two weeks, had come to fill a special place in her life.

More afraid of what she might see than of being caught, she had not dared to spy on his house again. Occasionally, she noticed fresh bruises on the boy's face and arms, and once a split lip, but she didn't see any more cigarette burns. She told herself that there was no need to report his parents to anybody. She wanted to believe that Neil had been right when he had said that they shouldn't interfere. But she was positive of one thing: The boy was happier now than he had been before she had made him her unofficial little brother.

In a sense, she had adopted him. Or had *he* adopted her? Whatever she called it, T.C. didn't want to think about what the boy would do when she moved to Oregon. She nursed a vague hope that she would be able to persuade Neil to get the boy from his mother and stepfather so that he could go to the farm with them.

This time, she didn't find him waiting on the other side of the fence. She looked up and down the street, worried that his parents might have locked him in, or beat him up so that he couldn't walk. Then she heard the chickens in the backyard squawking and crackling as if a fox had got loose in their midst. She ran around the house and found the boy cowering on the dirt in front of the plywood and chicken-wire cage, his arms over his head, quivering with terror. Apparently, he had tried to make friends with the hens and the ill-tempered birds had attacked him.

"It's okay," she said, coming up behind the boy. "They won't hurt you." She picked him up from the ground, but he broke away and darted around the house. She ran after him to the front of the house.

He looked angry, shaking his head and backing away. She didn't understand what had happened. She tried to take his hand, but he jerked away and crashed into the fence, letting out a snarling howl. Then he turned back toward her and she could see that his face was wet with tears. Rivulets ran through the dirt smeared over his face. His mouth opened and those strange, hoarse cries that she had heard when she first encountered him broke loose from his lips as he lunged forward and kicked her on the ankle. She swore and reached for him, but he hit her hand with his fist. He was stronger than she would have expected.

"You little devil!"

His fury grew as he fought, kicking and flailing at her. If any of the boys in the commune or at school had acted this way, she would have given him back the same, but she couldn't bring herself to strike at this kid, whatever he did to her.

"What is it?" she cried, "What's the matter?"

Those hideous sounds burst from his throat again, and he jabbed a finger through the air, pointing at her head. At last she understood.

"My hair! My hair! Is that it? You're mad because I cut off my hair?"

The girl dropped to her knees on the sidewalk and wrapped her arms around the small boy. He tried to twist out of her grasp, his skinny body eel-like within the circle of her arms, but she wouldn't let him go. Spittle dangled on the boy's lips and perspiration ran in muddy rivers down his flushed face. She pulled him close to her and hugged him tightly.

"I'm sorry. Is it that ugly?" She answered her own question with a nod. "I'm sorry I cut it." With one hand she pulled at the short locks of hair. "But it'll grow! My hair grows very fast!"

She didn't know if the boy understood her, or not, so she ran both of her hands through what was left of her hair, pulling at it until it was standing on end. The boy stopped fighting and stared at her head with huge eyes.

She hugged the boy and then reached into her pocket and pulled out the French bread roll and cheese. "Here!" she said, thrusting them into his hands.

He wiped his face with his sleeve and bit off a piece of the roll.

"I have an apple, too!" she said, showing it to him.

Together, the boy spreading bread and cheese crumbs

over his cheeks, the girl balancing the apple in her hand, they walked toward Telegraph Avenue. A pair of elderly joggers in yellow and red nylon shorts and white T-shirts ran past. Both of the men were about as old as Neil, but much thinner. One of them wore a sweatband around his head, keeping his gray hair out of his eyes. A college student on a motorcycle roared in the opposite direction, and an old Beatles tune sung by the BeeGees floated down from a second-story rooming house window. T.C. had never felt as close to anyone in her life as she did to the boy at this moment.

"I was stupid," she told him, "I got mad and lopped off my hair. Cutting off my nose to spite my face, that's what Malvina calls it. I wish I hadn't done it, but that's how I am. My parents weren't even surprised. They expect me to do dumb things." She paused and looked at the boy's narrow face. "Do you understand anything I'm saying? Do you ever understand me?"

They boy's expression remained unchanged as he chewed steadily on the roll and cheese.

"Never mind. Maybe I have enough money for an ice cream bar at Park and Shop. Do you want an ice cream bar?"

T.C.'s eyes were becoming blurry and she felt like a fool. Almost twelve years old and she was acting like a baby.

"Come on," she said. "I haven't got all day!" She gestured impatiently, and the boy trotted after her.

At first, T.C. tried to keep the boy her secret, but the others saw him hanging around. Jack joked that the kid had a crush on T.C. and Kevin chanted that she had a boyfriend, until Neil told them to lay off.

When school started, T.C. found it easier to get extra

food for her young friend. She slipped treats into her lunch bag and saved them for when she met him after school. Malvina noticed that T.C. was eating more, but assumed that it was because the girl was growing so fast. Then, one afternoon, she caught T.C. stuffing her pockets with cookies and raisins.

"T.C., do you have a tapeworm, or are you selling all that food to your friends?"

"What?"

T.C. looked up at Malvina's pale, lined face beneath the shaggy gray hair that appeared for all the world like a lopsided wig, and put on her most innocent expression. It didn't work.

"I've been watching you, T.C. I think you're smuggling food out to somebody. Is it that boy? That deaf and dumb boy you found here that day?" T.C. shrugged, but Malvina interpreted the silence as admission of guilt. "Listen to me, T.C., I'm not angry with you. I think it shows you've got a big heart, but you've got to think of the commune, too. We can't feed the whole transient population of Berkeley. It's expensive enough feeding ourselves. Do you realize that every cookie and raisin you steal—and it *is* stealing—from this kitchen hurts everybody else in this house? It makes our dream of getting to Oregon just a little bit further away. You know we don't waste anything. Every scrap is used. That's part of our life. If we had extra food, I'd be the first to say, 'Here, give it to that poor unfortunate tyke.' But we don't."

T.C. nodded and began taking the cookies and raisins from her pockets.

"Never mind that, T.C. Go ahead and give them to him, this time. But no more. Let his parents feed him. He's their responsibility, not yours."

T.C. nodded again and shuffled out the door. She found the boy waiting for her in the usual place.

He was always hanging around the neighborhood, looking out for her. Apparently, he didn't go to school. She wondered if he had ever gone.

A teacher would have noticed things, might have made trouble for his parents. Probably they had kept him away from schools and teachers and anybody else who might report them. They let the boy run wild, a little animal, and controlled him the way they would control an animal: with pain.

The week when T.C. began junior high school was also the week of her twelfth birthday.

She didn't have a real party, but her mother and father and some of the others gave her presents (mostly clothes for school) and that evening, after dinner, Malvina brought out a huge carob and honey cake with twelve candles on it and everybody sang "Happy Birthday."

After dinner, T.C. took a piece of the cake wrapped in a napkin for the boy.

He wasn't waiting by the gate or anyplace on the block that she could see. When he didn't show up after half an hour, she walked around to the street on which he lived.

She hoped that the boy might be outside, in front of his house, but she didn't see him. The duplex looked dark and empty. Weeds grew three and four feet tall in front of it. A jolt of panic hit her in the stomach. What if they had moved?

Those two, the mother and stepfather, might have taken the boy with them anyplace, who could say where, and she never would see him again. What would become of him?

She felt sick at the thought of the kid being starved and

battered with no one to give him affection, or a present.

It was *her* fault if anything had happened to him. She had been too chicken to do what should have been done. If anybody else had called her a coward, she would have socked him, but she accused herself, and felt that there was no punishment severe enough for her crime.

"If it's not too late," she told herself, standing in front of the rundown little duplex, "I'm going to do something to get him away from them, whether Neil or anybody else will help me, or not."

The door in the two-story house across the driveway opened and the bald, fat man T.C. had talked with before appeared, carrying what appeared to be a plastic bag of garbage. He looked over at her and frowned.

T.C. twisted her fingers together behind her back and approached him. "Those people still live there?"

"Who ya mean?"

"That boy and his mother—and that man, his stepfather." She pointed to the duplex. "Have they moved?"

The fat man clutched his bag of garbage to his belly, as if he expected T.C. to try to steal it.

"I'm a friend," said T.C.

The man stared at her with his little pig eyes and then shrugged his fleshy shoulders.

"I don't know. I ain't seen 'em for a while. Maybe they did move. Good riddance. That boy, that Caper Scanlon, I don't think he's right in the head. Sometimes, he was over there, howling like a dog. No normal kid makes noises like that. Not hour after hour. You ask me, that boy oughta be put away someplace."

The fat man shifted his sack of garbage in his arms and waddled around his house to his trash can.

T.C. glared after him, but didn't say any of the things she

was thinking. Now she knew the boy's name: Caper Scanlon!

But she was scared, too. Why had he been howling?

She ran around the side of the duplex, where the fat man wouldn't see her, and peered in the window. Except for a couple of chairs and a small table, the room seemed empty. The other window on that side of the house was covered with a tattered shade.

T.C. walked all around the duplex. Seeds from the tall weeds stuck to her socks. Both units appeared to be unoccupied. The weeds in the backyard were taller and thicker than those in the front. Paint was peeling from the stucco walls and an old swingset frame with no swings stood rusting among the weeds.

She sat on the loose boards of the back step to pick the stickers from her socks and try to think about what to do. Even if they still lived here, she didn't know what she would say to either of the adults. Ask if Caper could play?

She didn't think that anybody was in the house, but she was afraid to knock on the door. She didn't want to risk tangling with that guy she had watched through the window. He was crippled, but he was strong, and she had seen what he was capable of doing.

"So what," she decided, "I'm gonna do it!'

She jumped up and hammered on the back door with her fist. The noise crashed like a gunshot through the afternoon air.

Startled by her own daring, she stared at the weathered door, waiting for it to open and bring her face to face with either the woman or that hairy-chested, crippled man.

The door didn't open. She wasn't sure if she felt relieved or disappointed.

Kicking at the gray wood of the low railing, she abandoned the back porch and picked her way through the weeds around the side of the duplex. She had reached the front corner of the house when she heard a car door slam. She hesitated and then crouched among the wild grass and dandelions.

Peeking from behind the dry, tangled growth, T.C. saw the woman pushing the man up the walk in his wheelchair. He gestured angrily with his big hands.

"The little bastard is *your* kid, I don't give a damn what you do with him, as long as you get him out of my hair."

The woman's reply was muffled by the sound of a passing delivery truck, and then the front door opened and closed.

So they hadn't gone! The boy—Caper—was in the house, right now. Maybe they weren't letting him out anymore. Maybe they were afraid of being discovered.

Crouching in the weeds at the corner of the house, T.C. imagined all kinds of horrible scenes behind the walls of the duplex.

I should go straight to the police, she told herself, and describe what I know about Caper and those people. But no adult would believe her. If Neil wasn't willing to help, nobody else would, either. And, for some reason that she didn't understand, it would have seemed a defeat to run crying to a grown-up.

"Be self-reliant," Neil preached to the kids in the commune. Well, that's what she wanted to be. Except that she didn't know what to do.

One thing was certain: She didn't want to be found hiding in the weeds.

It occurred to her that all she had to do was hang around, watching the house, until the man and woman both left again. Then she could knock and Caper would let her in and she could get him to go away with her.

She would help him to hide. If necessary she'd hide with him.

The idea didn't frighten her. In fact, it was appealing. To run away and hide, to become free of all grown-ups: didn't every boy and girl dream of it? Some of her favorite books, like *Huckleberry Finn* and *Catcher in the Rye*, were about kids who ran away and had adventures. They were about boys, because girls weren't supposed to want to run off and have dangerous and exciting lives. But that was just one more way in which adults were wrong about girls. She wanted to be free to do what she pleased and she knew that whatever happened she wouldn't be afraid.

And she would have Caper. They would have each other.

There were ways to live. Kids didn't need big houses and furniture and cars. Kids knew what was important. They could get by with almost nothing. Like those teenagers she saw in Berkeley, who traveled all across the United States, even around the world, with no other possessions than a backpack and a bedroll.

The more she thought about it, the more certain she was that she and Caper could manage together. All she had to do was get him away from those people who thought it was fun to hurt him.

Keeping low, so that no one inside the house who chanced to look out the window would notice her, T.C. hurried across the small, weed-choked side yard to the street. Not glancing back, she ran between parked cars, jogged across the street, and ducked behind a Volkswagen van.

Now, her heart pounding in her chest, she dared to look at the duplex. It appeared no different than before: just a tacky little house, rundown, a neighborhood eyesore. She thought how strange it was that walls could hide so much. It always had seemed that a house was just a house, but really it was a collection of walls behind which people's lives took place. They were like stage sets with the curtains down, and you hardly ever got a glimpse of the plays being acted on them.

The boy was behind those ugly little walls. It was because of those walls that the man and woman were able to get away with everything that they did. And she would have to hide here, staring at those walls, until she could get Caper away from there.

She didn't want to arouse suspicion by prowling around like a thief. If anybody passed by she would have to act natural. One advantage she had was that people suspected boys of being up to no good before they suspected girls.

Soon they would be expecting her at home, but she'd make up an excuse to come out after dinner. She could always say that she was going to the library. And she'd return tomorrow, and the day after, and as long as it took. Once she decided to do something, nobody could be as stubborn as Teresa Carlotta Helprin.

She knew that the flaw in her plan was that she couldn't watch the duplex twenty-four hours a day. She had to interrupt her vigil with school and with meals and duties at home.

Whenever T.C. had a chance, she stood across the street, pretending to wait for a bus, or hiding behind a parked car or pickup truck. Nobody said anything, but she thought that a few people walking past gave her some strange looks.

Several times, T.C. saw the woman come and go, but the man remained in the house. She never did get a glimpse of Caper. A week crawled by without an opportunity to find the boy alone. Finally, she saw the man wheel himself out of the house and up the block and around the corner. An hour or so later, he returned and the woman left again. It looked to T.C. as if she was crying.

The woman didn't look cruel. What made her mistreat her son? How could anybody deliberately hurt someone else, especially someone small and helpless? T.C. didn't understand it. There had to be something haywire about people like that. Something wrong with their brains.

Late one afternoon, when T.C. had been watching the house for more than a week, the door opened and the woman wheeled the man out in his chair. They were both dressed up more than T.C. had ever seen them before. The woman was wearing high heels and a silky, flowered dress and had curled her hair. Big, floppy plastic earrings dangled from her earlobes. The man wore polyester slacks and a shiny blue jacket over a flowered, open-collared shirt. A gold chain glinted on his hairy chest. The woman pushed the man's chair to the street. They looked around, as if they expected to see somebody waiting for them, and then the woman opened the car door and helped the man into the front seat. He hoisted himself up on his huge arms, balancing between the car seat and the wheelchair, and she guided him into place. Wherever they were going, dressed up like that, T.C. hoped that they would be gone for a good long time.

The car jerked away from the curb and shot off down the block. T.C. waited until it turned the corner before she ran across the street. She crashed through the weeds, around the side of the duplex, and up the two low steps to the back door.

"Caper!" she called. "Can you hear me? Let me in! It's T.C.!" She pounded on the flimsy door with her fist, but heard no response from inside the house. She kicked at the door and hit at the glass windowpane. She tried to peek in, but the windows were covered with shades or heavy plastic curtains. One window had newspaper taped over it.

Maybe Caper really is deaf, she thought.

She decided to break into the house. She found a good-sized rock near the back porch, stood back, and hurled it at the window on the door.

The shattering of the glass sounded to her ears like the firing of a cannon. She expected to see all of the neighbors running over to find out what was happening.

"If they call the cops," she decided, crouching in the weeds by the rusty swing set frame, "I'll tell them all about Caper."

But nobody appeared. After a few more minutes, she emerged from the weeds, ignoring the stickers clinging to her socks and scratching at her legs. Carefully, she reached through the broken window and unlocked the back door. The bottom of the door crunched over broken glass when she pushed it open.

Crusted pots and pans, tin cans half full of rotting food, slimy dishes, glasses and cups with cigarette butts swimming in a half inch of disgusting liquid, and emptied beer cans and wine bottles cluttered the kitchen counter and table top. Grease had spattered the walls and mingled with the dust on top of the old black and white enameled stove. A faded, grease-stained, two-year-old calender adorned with the ragged picture of a naked woman hung askew above the refrigerator.

T.C. picked her way through the dishes scattered over the floor and around piles of TV dinner aluminum trays on which the remains of meatloaf and pork and bean and turkey dinners had congealed, and pushed open the door to the front of the house.

The place smelled of rotten food and dampness. Great brown stains wandered like maps over the flowered wallpaper.

"Hello?" she called. "Caper?"

In the living room, she found a birdcage, the bottom of which was covered with droppings and seed hulls, but it was occupied by a twisted beer can instead of a bird. Other beer cans balanced on top of the television set and marched like soldiers across the battered plywood coffee table and across the worn linoleum floor. The first bedroom, with only a bed for furniture and a few clothes scattered over an open suitcase and across the floor, looked as if people had been temporarily camping in it. T.C. hesitated at the door to the second bedroom, wishing that she didn't have to look behind it.

I don't want to know, she thought. But she had to know.

Her hand turned the knob, but when she tried to nudge open the door, it resisted. She discovered, several inches above her head, a sliding bolt. She clicked it open and the door swung wide.

T.C. blinked, waiting for her eyes to adjust to the darkness. The single window in the room was covered with several layers of newspapers. There was no furniture. The room smelled of urine. Then she saw a pile of rags in the corner, near what was probably a closet door. The pile of rags moved.

"Caper!"

She hurried over and knelt beside him. The stink made her gag. Curled in a ball, Caper held himself and whimpered.

T.C. searched the walls for a light switch, her hands slapping the bulgy, damp wallpaper like those of a blind person. When she found the switch, it proved useless: no bulb in the socket.

She banged at the window, ripping at the newspapers with her fingers. Like a cruel spotlight, the afternoon sun sliced through the dirty glass into the tiny room.

A prison; this room was a prison. They hadn't even let him go to the bathroom. What kind of people were they?

Kneeling beside the boy, T.C. turned him over. It wasn't easy, but she managed to keep herself from being sick.

His face was swollen and bruised, his lip split and bruised, one blackened eye swollen shut. Welts and deep abrasions covered with crusted blood merged forehead with scalp. Sections of hair seemed to have been yanked out in handfuls. He covered his eyes with a skinny arm and she saw more bruises and those nasty little burns that she now knew were produced by a lighted cigarette. There were so many of them that she couldn't count them. Less than two weeks since she had seen the boy, but she could hardly recognize him. They must have been deliberately starving him.

She cradled the boy's scarred, wounded head in her lap and tried to decide what to do. Call the police? A hospital?

She didn't want to get mixed up with a lot of adults. They would take Caper away from her, put him in a hospital or an orphanage or foster home, where people might be mean to him again. She would *kill* anybody who tried to hurt this boy.

But how wounded was he? She had heard about intenal injuries that could be worse than those a person could see. She didn't want to take any chances. She wanted the boy to get well.

And his parents: Someday, she thought, they should be punished, tortured the way they had tortured this kid. But first she had to get him away, before they came back.

"Can you sit up?" She tried to support him with her arms. He made funny little bubbling noises in his throat, and his head flopped forward. He was a rag doll, with no backbone. "Please!" she cried. "You've *got* to!"

Holding him beneath the armpits, she propped up his almost weightless body, leaning it against her. She pulled a Kleenex from her pocket and wiped off his face, and then dragged him across the filthy floor and braced him against the wall. Large, ugly insects scurried across the worn, stained linoleum, hiding among the dust balls in the corners and disappearing through invisible cracks around the floorboards.

She ran to the bathroom, snatched a rust-stained towel from a doorknob, and wet part of it in the basin. With it, she washed the boy's face and scrubbed his hands. Tenderly, she tried to clean the sores and cuts on his forehead and scalp. He jerked away and stared at T.C. as if he didn't recognize her. His tongue rolled around in his mouth.

"Are you thirsty? Is that it?"

In the kitchen, she found a glass, rinsed it out, and filled it with water from the tap.

"Here!" She held the glass to his lips and helped him to drink. Water spilled from his mouth, but he swallowed enough of it to revive him somewhat. "More? No, there's no time. We've got to get out of here. Please, Caper, it's *me*. Don't you recognize me? It's T.C. Your friend."

His head still flopped on his neck, but his eyes seemed to focus more clearly. Maybe he did know who she was, as well as he could know anything.

She looked around the room for clean clothes. On the closet floor, she found a T-shirt somewhat less revolting than the one he was wearing. She peeled the old one off him, exposing a pattern of welts and bruises across his chest and back. His back looked like the lumpy hide of a reptile, and his ribs pressed through his almost transparent, pale skin. She hurled the filthy T-shirt into the corner and pulled the other one over his head. He flinched with pain when she shoved his arms through the sleeves, and she saw that his joints were swollen.

The stink from the boy's trousers was foul, but there didn't seem to be a single garment left in either the room or the closet. Somebody had deliberately destroyed or thown away his clothes. In fact, it looked as if somebody had been trying to remove all traces of his existence. There was nothing in the house to suggest that a nine-year-old boy lived in it. Nothing but the one T-shirt she had discovered in the back of the closet.

"I'll have to take you as you are, and get you some clean clothes later. Come on."

She lifted him to his feet, leaning against her. He was so light that she could have carried him. Slowly, she maneuvered him through the house to the back door.

"Please, God," she prayed, "don't let them come home now!"

The boy showed little understanding of what was happening, but he moved along as well as he could, not fighting her. They paused a moment on the back porch, the boy like a small sparrow in her arms, then she eased him down the two plank steps into the yard.

Outside, it was harder going. He stumbled over uneven places in the ground and fell among the weeds, as if he had forgotten how to walk. She was terrified of being discovered by his mother and stepfather. For the first time in all of this, she felt like a child, vulnerable, at the mercy of adults. Only a determination born of rage kept her going.

T.C. hugged the boy, whispering to him, trying to help him find the strength to move, trying with all of her determination to *will* strength into him.

She dragged him to his feet, draped his arm over her shoulder, and compelled him to move forward. Crushing the weeds, they progressed inch by inch, through the yard, around the side of the house, until they reached the corner of the duplex nearest the street. Every time she accidentally touched one of his wounds, Caper flinched and moaned with pain.

Which way to go? Which direction would be the safest?

There was no time for deliberations. She dragged him along the pavement, across the street, along the sidewalk. Each time he groaned, she shared the pain, but she had to be merciless if they were to succeed in their escape. A car slowed as it passed, and T.C. felt as if her heart would stop, but when she dared to look up she saw that it was not Caper's mother and stepfather.

The journey couldn't have lasted more than two or three minutes, but it seemed like an hour before they reached the corner. When she stopped to catch her breath and rest her aching muscles, Caper slipped from her grasp and fell to the pavement. His only reaction was a faint whimper.

Just then, she saw the familiar dark sedan dead ahead. she recognized its unpainted, rusty front fender. She dropped to the ground beside Caper, hoping they were hidden by the Volkswagen bug parked at the curb.

The sedan passed them, turned the corner, and drove up to the weathered duplex in the middle of the block. She could hear the car doors open and close. She crawled around and watched the woman setting up the folding wheelchair and helping the man out of the car and into the chair. He made a gesture of impatience and the woman bent over him, as if apologizing. She pushed the man up to the front door and fumbled in her purse for a key. Even half a block away, T.C. could hear the woman's husband swearing at her. Finally, the door was open and the woman steered the chair into the house.

The moment the door closed, T.C. grabbed at Caper and pulled him upright. "Come on!" she said.

Half-running in a lopsided jog, her arms about to break off, T.C. dragged the boy around another corner, toward the pair of shingled houses in which the commune lived.

She pulled him down the driveway, toward the rear of the house—it was too risky to take him through the front gate—and prayed that nobody would be in the backyard. All she needed was to run into Jack or Kevin shooting baskets or her father messing around with his collection of bolts and nuts. But this time luck was with her. She dragged the boy into the garage, past the pickup truck parked there, to a door at the rear. Years ago, the garage had been a carriage house, and the little room at the back had probably been used to store harnesses and trappings; now, it was filled with junk, but it did have an old sofa in it, and she had already brought out a couple of blankets and some food.

The boy fell onto the dusty, broken-down sofa and covered his scabby head with one thin arm, as if trying to ward off blows. T.C. dug the blankets out of a box of rubbish and covered him. Standing motionless beside the sofa, she listened for sounds outside the garage and shrouded her face with her hands. The last hour had been almost too much for her.

How easy it would be, she thought, to go up to the house and tell her parents everything. Instantly, the responsibility would be lifted from her shoulders. She would be an ordinary twelve-year-old girl again, worried about only homework and household chores. It would be so easy.

When she left the garage she saw Neil's bulky, bearded form on the back porch of the house. At first, she thought that he must be watching her, but then she saw that he was scraping down the railing, preparing to repaint it. Bits of dry old paint flaked off in showers around him, falling like snow on the steps and earth below the railing.

Okay, she decided, one more time: She would give him a chance to prove that he believed everything that he preached.

She strode to the edge of the porch and looked up at him, hands on hips. "Neil?"

"Hi, T.C. Want to help me scrape off the old paint?"

She shook her head. "I want to ask you a question."

"Okay, I'm listening." He did not stop scraping the aged paint from the gray wood.

"Neil, do you remember what I told you about that boy? How his parents—his mother and stepfather, really—were so mean to him?"

"You still worried about that?"

"Listen, Neil. I went back and I found out it's worse even than I said before. They're starving him. They lock him up in his room, and don't let him go to the toilet. And they beat him. They hurt him on purpose, like it's a game. Please, can't we adopt him? Can't we make the police take him away from them and let him live with us? I promise I'll work hard, so he won't be in anybody's way. Please, we've got to do something for him, before they kill him."

Neil looked up at T.C. "Listen to yourself, T.C. Do you realize how absurd you sound? You've got to learn not to dramatize life so much. I don't doubt that some of what you're telling me is true, but you *are* exaggerating it, aren't you?"

"No, I'm not. Neil . . ."

But he wasn't listening. His head bent down, close to his

work, he asked her if she was concentrating on her classes this year. "You don't want to let your imagination interfere with what's important."

T.C. turned her back on him. She walked around to the side of the garage and slipped in, through the small door hidden among the ivy tendrils hanging down from the steeply sloped roof. She found Caper as she had left him, huddled in his blanket like an abandoned infant.

Standing among the shelves of ancient preserves, surrounded by dusty, long-unused machinery and forgotten tools, the twelve-year-old girl looked down on the boy and felt a tenderness toward him that she never had experienced before. It was similar to feelings she had felt toward puppies and young kittens, but more intense. Partly, it was because he was so helpless and dependent on her, as a kitten is dependent upon its owner, and partly it was because they had gone through so much together, but even more this feeling was based on her conviction that they shared the future. Whatever happened, she believed with a fearful certainty, they would experience it together.

4

September is a warm month in Berkeley, but still T.C. worried about Caper staying all night in the garage. Several times she woke up, afraid for him. What if he was cold, hungry, afraid? She wanted to go out to him, but she knew if she stirred she might wake one of the girls in the other beds.

She waited until dawn before she pulled on her bathrobe and slippers and inched her way out of the long, second-floor bedroom. Five-year-old Wendy rolled over and mumbled in her sleep, but T.C. was out of the room before the little girl could wake up and discover her.

T.C. hesitated at the top of the stairs, kneeling on the window seat to look down into the yard below. The morning was pink and dove gray and very still. As she knelt there, the rising chirrup and twittering of the birds signaled the beginning of the day. Two sparrows appeared on the patch of grass beside the concrete area where the boys played basketball. Their heads darted up and down, looking for breakfast, then twitched sideways, as if to keep an eye out for enemies. T.C. slipped off the window seat and padded silently down the stairs to the back door.

The morning air slapped her like the chill from an open refrigerator. She ran across the yard, scattering the sparrows and a robin or two, and heaved open the garage door. Squeezing past the pickup truck and the Volkswagen van now parked beside it, she made her way to the little door at the rear of the garage. A sudden fear that he might not be there choked her as she turned the knob.

She jerked open the door on its rusty, stubborn hinges, and peered into the back room. He lay tightly curled in the blankets on the sagging sofa.

T.C. inched between the old wooden workbench and the back of the sofa until she could see his face. His hair was pasted over his forehead and the blanket was pulled up over his nose, but his eyes glittered in the dim morning light angling in through the small window above the sofa. Motionless, he stared up at her.

"Are you hungry?" she asked. "Thirsty?"

His smell reminded her that she still hadn't found him clean trousers. It had been difficult enough trying to take care of his wounds last night. She had snitched bandaids and ointment from the medicine cabinet in the upstairs bathroom, and had brought down a towel and some warm water. When she had set about trying to clean the sores on his back and arms and head, he had resisted with what little strength he had left, kicking and flailing and even biting her. But she had held him down and, even if she hadn't got him very clean, had managed to smear some of the ointment onto the sores on his arms and back and to pour iodine onto the deeper cuts. She had had to cover his mouth with the towel to smother his yelp when she looked after the wound on his scalp.

"I'll be right back," she promised, "I'll get more food and something to drink. And clean pants, too. One of the boys must have some jeans that'll fit you."

Caper's head lolled sideways, his eyes staring vacantly into the shadowed corner of the room. Then, slowly, it turned toward her, until she could see, illuminated by a narrow shaft of light from the window, his dark eyes focused on her.

In the laundry room, T.C. dug through piled clothes until she found a pair of jeans that seemed about right. Then she ran to the kitchen, snitched a carton of milk and a bag of cookies, and hurried back to the garage. It wasn't much of a meal, but she didn't have time to look for more. Several of the adults had to be up early to get to their jobs. They would soon be down to fix themselves breakfast.

"Here," she said, setting the cookies and milk on the workbench. "But change your pants first, okay?"

He stared at her.

She held out the jeans. He didn't move.

"Want me to help you?"

She jerked back the blankets, exposing his scrawny, bunched-up arms and legs. His eyes were huge with fear.

"You're scared of me, aren't you?" She sat down beside him and wrapped her arms around his skinny body, hugging him against her chest. "You don't have to be scared anymore. I promise you, you don't ever have to be scared again. I'm going to take care of you."

She rocked him in her arms, whispering to him, telling him that everything was going to be all right. Then she pulled the foul trousers off and tugged the fresh jeans onto him. They were a little too large, but they didn't stink. She sat him up on the sofa, tucked the blankets around him, and gave him the cookies. Crumbs exploded around him like confetti on New Year's Eve, but eating the cookies seemed to make him feel better. When he was thirsty, she helped him drink out of the milk carton. Finally, he finished eating and she told him that she had to leave.

Until she knew for a fact that he was deaf, she intended to talk to him as if he could hear her. "Be quiet, won't you? Don't make any noise at all. I'll be back."

He looked at her, but gave no indication that he understood. Slowly, his eyes closed, his head fell forward, and he slept again.

Well, she thought, if he's asleep he can't make any noise.

She managed to get upstairs and into the bathroom before the other girls discovered that she was missing from her bed. She flushed the toilet and tromped back to the bedroom, yawning loudly.

"Lazybones," she said to Wendy. The five-year-old stretched and waved at T.C. with her rag doll. "Where you been, T.C.?"

"I've already had breakfast!"

"Fibber!" Wendy waggled her finger at T.C. "You just been to the toilet!"

T.C. grinned and began to put on her clothes for the day.

When T.C. sat down at the table with the others for breakfast, she hadn't made up her mind to run away, but after listening to her father talking about his bolt and nut collection and Neil reciting his plans for the farm in Oregon, she realized that she had no choice. She wondered if anybody could tell what was going on in her mind. Was her secret visible on her face?

Malvina asked her husband if they would have a modern kitchen in Oregon. "Eventually," Neil told her, "but at first we may have to rough it." Malvina nodded and began collecting the plates from the breakfast table. She was used to roughing it.

For the first time, T.C. felt sorry for Malvina. The old woman must have had to endure a lot from that husband of hers. But T.C. wasn't married to him, or to the commune. She could break away. And she had a reason now.

As soon as she finished eating, T.C. dashed off to the attic storeroom where supplies such as sleeping bags and backpacks were kept in promiscuous, if untidy, piles. She would have to carry everything for both of them, but Caper was so small that they could share a sleeping bag. They would take only one backpack, she decided, and live from day to day.

T.C. hadn't thought out what running away really meant, but it seemed simple enough to her. She deliberately avoided thinking about where she would go and what she would do to survive. If she let herself dwell on specifics, she might lose her courage.

She did think about Caper Scanlon as she dug through the backpacks and bedrolls in the attic. She didn't believe that he was retarded. Anybody who had been brutalized the way he had been would act the way he did. She would probably never know all the horrors that had been done to him.

T.C. lugged the backpack and sleeping bag down to the garage, then slipped into the back room and dropped her burden on the end of the old sofa. Caper looked up at her. She guessed that he was glad to see her. There are other ways of communicating than words, she though. They would get along okay.

T.C. knew she had to run away—it was too risky keeping Caper in the back of the garage. But she couldn't think where to take him. She didn't have any friends whom she could trust with a secret like this.

Unless . . .the Orange Man. It was just possible that *he* would help her. They were friends, weren't they? He liked her. Maybe he would do it for her.

She peered out of the garage in time to see her father leap on his bicycle and shoot off down the driveway, late as usual. He would pedal like crazy all the way to the campus, park his bike, run two flights up to his classroom, and, in a sweat, apologize to his students for five minutes before launching into the morning's lecture. She had heard all about it when some of his students had visited the commune. Her father was famous for being late to everything. He didn't even realize that people laughed at him.

T.C. crept down the long driveway, staying against the house, until she reached the street. Anyone who saw her would ask why she wasn't in school, and she didn't have a ready answer.

Soon, she was making her way down Telegraph Avenue, through the morning crowds, past the sidewalk salesmen setting out their wares, to the campus. On the plaza by the student union, the food vendors were setting up their stands. The juice wagon was wheeled into position while she waited for the traffic light, and the doughnut lady opened her stall for business. T.C. wandered through the mob of students and faculty and secretaries and staff hurrying to classrooms and offices.

She bought herself an apple and sat on the edge of Ludwig's Fountain munching it and watching the people. A motorized wheelchair maneuvered through the crowd toward her. She jumped up, ready to run, before she saw that the long-haired man in the chair did not look at all like Caper's stepfather. She sank back onto the edge of the brick fountain and resumed watching the people.

Then she saw the Orange Man.

T.C. finished her apple and dropped the core into a trash can. He didn't notice her even when she stood directly in front of him. Fumbling in his net bag of oranges, he muttered to himself and scratched at his goatee. Then he looked up.

"Hey" he said.

"Hi." T.C. accepted the orange that he offered her.

"Thanks." She peered up into his face, but saw that he was looking inward, toward a secret landscape within his own head.

"I'm not crazy," he said, at last. "They want to lock me up, but I'm saner than they are. They'll see. When they're dead, and I'm still alive, they'll see."

T.C. tugged at his sleeve, trying to make him pay attention to her. "I need your help. Listen, won't you? You've got to help me."

His eyes wandered down to her and seemed to focus on her face. Perhaps he was caught by her plain features, cobwebbed with anxiety, perhaps he saw nothing at all. She rushed into her story, telling about Caper. He nodded and shrugged, twitching occasionally, as if with sorrow, and now and then interrupting her to hand somebody an orange. He made no comment until she was finished and then he nodded his fuzzy head and observed: "If folks ate more oranges they wouldn't do things like that."

T.C. could not hold back her disappointment. "Oh!" she groaned.

"No, it's true. You see, they're not healthy, and people who aren't healthy hurt each other. I got it all worked out."

"Yeah. I know. But I need help. Oranges aren't enough, this time. I need somebody to let Caper stay with him for a few days."

The Orange Man tilted his head and scratched at his skimpy beard again. He seemed not to understand what she was saying. "They want to lock me up. Did you know that?"

"Listen to me!" cried T.C. "Can Caper stay with you?"

"*Me*? Oh, no. Nobody stays with me. I live alone. All alone. I can't live with other people. Just me and my oranges. We don't want anybody else. We won't let them lock us up with other people." He shook his fuzzy head.

"But—"

"No. Impossible. Oh, no . . . never." The Orange Man jerked his head back and forth and shuffled a few steps away from T.C. He looked frightened.

"I didn't mean to upset you," said T.C.

"I ain't upset." He lunged forward and thrust a couple of oranges at a pair of passersby. They accepted the oranges, but smirked at each other.

"I ain't upset," he repeated. "I know they won't lock me up."

T.C. saw that it was hopeless. "Goddamn it!" she shouted. "I thought you were my friend! I'm in trouble and you won't even help me!"

He jerked around, his eyes big with surprise, and stared at her. He looked as if he was going to cry, but she didn't care. She was too angry, too disappointed. She stomped away.

He hollered after her: "Remember: the human body needs two dozen oranges every day!"

T.C. didn't respond. She left him standing near the big round fountain in the middle of the plaza, balancing a pair of oranges in each hand, holding them out like golden nuggets to the passersby.

After she crossed the bridge over Strawberry Creek, she sat down on a bench and held her chin in her hand, staring at the leaf-strewn pavement. She felt rotten. She had been unfair to the Orange Man. He had been trying to tell her something, too, but she had been too caught up in her own problem to listen. She had cursed at him and hurt his feelings, and she felt guilty. He was like a child, really, and you weren't supposed to go around shouting at little kids and making them cry.

And she still didn't know what to do with Caper. Where do I go, now? Who is left?

She waited until the coast was clear and then ran down the drive to the garage. Only a pair of black grease stains on the concrete floor remained where the pickup truck and van had been. Had anyone discovered Caper while getting into the truck and van?

T.C. pushed open the dusty door and focused her eyes in the half-light of the storeroom. The boy sat on the sofa, shoving something into his mouth. He had found the food that she had hidden behind the sofa: some candy bars, a couple of bananas, and a can of Coke. When he saw her, he shoved the Coke behind him and tried to hide the remains of a Baby Ruth.

"I'm not going to take it away from you." T.C. sat beside the boy and opened the Coke for him. "I'm on your side." She turned his head so that he could see her mouth. "Understand? I'm on your side."

He snatched the Coke and poured it into his open mouth, dribbling it down his chin and over his shirtfront.

"What am I going to *do* with you?" She sighed.

He gurgled, spilling Coke over the sofa and blankets.

"If nobody else will help us," she told him, "I guess we'll have to stand on our own two feet. Or four feet."

On her way to the campus, she had discarded his stinking trousers. The only clothes he had now were the shirt he was wearing and the pants she had borrowed. She would have to borrow some more clothes for him, including a pair of shoes. He needed a jacket, too. That might not be so easy.

There were a lot of things to consider, if she was going to take care of somebody besides herself. She wasn't used to thinking of anybody else before T.C. Helprin. She was discovering how much more complicated life became if you stopped to put another human's existence before your own.

But, at the same time, T.C. never had been as happy as she was at this minute. She was tired and scared and confused, but she felt a sense of fulfillment. And she was a bit triumphant, too, as if she had been victorious over the tribe of adults that ran the world.

Then there was the problem of money. She had no idea how much she would need, or where she'd get it, but she knew that it was a question she would have to confront, and soon.

She knelt on the sofa with Caper, took the empty Coke can out of his hands, wiped his face with a Kleenex tissue from her pocket, and held him close to her. She was still shocked by how thin he was. It was like embracing a skeleton.

"Uhhnnnh . . ."

An awful noise: Did it mean that he was happy or sad? The nasal sound broke off in a fit of coughing, and she pounded him on his scrawny back.

He collapsed beneath the weight of her pounding, his head rolling to the side. Her hand stopped in midair, as she realized with horror that he thought she was punishing him.

"Oh, no!" she cried, hugging him again. "I'm not mad at you. I'm not hitting you. I would never do that!" She rocked back and forth with him, as if he were an oversized doll on her lap. He was pliant as a creature made of rags and sawdust, but she had no way of knowing if she was making contact with him.

"I can't stay here all day," she whispered, at last. "I've got to fill the backpack. I have to go up to the house." She tried to explain to him what was going to happen. "I'll be back in a little while."

T.C. gave him a quick squeeze and jumped off the old sofa. The springs boinged loudly and pushed against the worn brown fabric. At the door, she paused, put her finger to her lips, and then hurried away.

She wanted to have everything ready before the other kids got home from school. It wouldn't take long for them to become suspicious if they spied her hiking back and forth from the garage. She wasn't worried that Jack or Kevin or the others would hurt Caper. They could be obnoxious, but they weren't mean. She was scared that they'd tell Neil, however. There seemed to be an unwritten law in the commune forbidding secrets. And a secret like this one! The boys would break their necks trying to be the first to tattle.

T.C. got inside the house without anybody noticing her, slipped past the kitchen, listened at the laundry room door, and darted inside. She was in luck. The freshly washed and dried laundry was sitting in neat stacks, waiting to be carried upstairs. It took her only a moment to find a good long-sleeved shirt and another pair of pants for Caper. She hesitated, decided that he needed underwear, found some shorts and a T-shirt that looked about right, snatched a couple of pairs of socks and a pair of sneakers she found on the floor, and rolled everything together into a compact ball that she could carry under her arm.

It wasn't as easy getting out of the house as it had been getting in. She could hear somebody working in the kitchen. She waited for several minutes behind the half-open laundry room door and then ran down the hall, through the door, across the back porch, down the stairs, and across the yard. She didn't slow down until she was inside the garage. Collapsing against the aged plank wall, she clutched the clothes to her heaving chest and listened for the sound of footsteps outside. When she heard no one else crossing the yard or calling her name, she decided that, so far, she was home safe.

"Told you I wouldn't be long!" she said, as she pushed open the door to the workshop. Then she saw that the sofa was empty. She dropped the clothes on the battered upholstery and looked up and down the length of the small, cramped room. Had he run away, or had someone found him?

Then she saw him curled up beneath the heavy-legged rustic workbench across from the sofa. He scooted backward, like a crab, into the shadows, cobwebs tangling in his hair, his knees and hands leaving trails in the dust on the concrete floor.

"Caper! What is it? Did somebody come in?" She crouched in front of the workbench. "Don't be afraid. Nobody's going to hurt you."

Rigid, between the workbench supports, he peered at her. Didn't he trust her? She sensed that she mustn't pressure him. She returned to the sofa and sat down; a broken spring in the cushion jabbed at her backside, but she hardly noticed it. She waited to see what Caper would do.

He watched her with his big, shadowed eyes. She pretended to be examining the clothes that she had brought from the house. She held up the T-shirt, admired it, and set it beside her, then held up the sneakers and looked at them as if they were the best sneakers ever touched by human hands. She was aware of him inching forward in the dust. Finally, he crawled out from under the workbench. He looked so young. She had guessed his age at nine, but he might be eight or seven. She knew nothing about him, not even his birthday. And if he couldn't or wouldn't talk, she'd never know.

"What scared you?" She spoke slowly, as if she were trying to teach a foreigner the English language. He climbed on the sofa and curled up like a cat on the end farthest from her.

T.C. reviewed her plan. It wouldn't take long to pack some clothes. The most important thing was money. She had already given that some thought. In her secret savings she had maybe twenty dollars, but that wouldn't last long. If she had had time, she might have raised more by selling the few possessions that were hers alone, but now she had no choice but to steal the money.

Still watching Caper at his end of the worn sofa, she considered the possibilities. Most of the kids had their own little savings put away. It would be easy to rob their piggy (or Snoopy or Winnie the Pooh) banks, but she couldn't bring herself to take money from other kids. If she asked her parents for money, they'd want to know why she wanted it, and if she stole if from them, she'd feel rotten. That left the commune. If she "borrowed" fifty dollars from the commune, at least she wouldn't be taking it from an individual. No one person would suffer.

If she was going to "borrow" it, she had better do it before she lost her nerve and before people started coming home from work and school.

Neil kept an emergency fund of several hundred dollars in a box in his desk. It was the policy of the commune that anybody (meaning any adult, of course) could help himself to some of the money at any time, leaving an IOU in the box. In the six and more years of the commune's existence no one had taken advantage of the emergency fund. Not a penny had ever been unaccounted for. Some of the early members who had dropped out had stolen food and supplies, portable radios and binoculars and other personal property, but even they had been too intimidated by Neil's moral code to violate the honor system of the emergency fund.

From the garage door, T.C. saw Malvina back the commune's old Dodge coupe out of the gravel driveway, crushing half a dozen iris on either side before she got the car onto the street. This was T.C.'s opportunity. She ran across the back yard to the porch, slipped into the house, and darted past the kitchen to the downstairs bathroom. Her mother was probably in the house someplace, but if she was careful, she would be able to dodge her. The odds were that her mom would either be cleaning upstairs or working in the kitchen. Her mother was the only person T.C. knew who enjoyed housecleaning. Even Malvina admitted that she hated chores such as vacuuming and dusting and scrubbing woodwork.

T.C. didn't hear any activity on the first floor, so she crept out of her hiding place and tiptoed down the hall to the library. Carefully sliding back the double doors, T.C. peered into the room.

Seventy-five years ago, when the house was new, the library had been an elegant room. The carved wood decorations around the bookcases, the heavy redwood mantel, and the bay window all suggested a former grandeur, but now they were chipped and battered and the furnishings were secondhand. The large-patterned carpet looked discontented in the shabby, haphazard room. The sofa was not in much better repair than the old one abandoned in the garage workshop. There were also a pair of slipcovered overstuffed chairs, a few mismatched straightback chairs, a round oak table that would have been handsome if somebody had taken the time and trouble to refinish it, and Neil's massive desk. Only the desk was a genuinely fine piece of furniture, and it was buried under mountains of papers and books.

T.C. tiptoed across the worn oriental carpet to the desk, her heart beating like a drum roll to her chest. She stopped and took a deep breath. She felt sick.

"I can't do it."

She stared hopelessly at the oak desk, at the stacks of newspapers and letters and paperback books. An unfinished letter jutted like a wide flat tongue out of the old typewriter. Neil loved that antique Underwood and refused to part with it, although nobody else could make it function.

How could she steal from the commune, the only home she had known since she was six years old? And Neil. What would Neil think of her? She didn't care about the others so much, but she couldn't bear to have Neil think of her as a thief.

"I've *got* to do it!"

She commanded her legs to move around the desk and peered past Neil's ancient leather-covered chair to the double rows of drawers. She knew precisely in which drawer the money box was kept. She even knew which corner of the drawer.

Suddenly she heard footsteps, then the double doors sliding on their tracks. Was it her mother? She hadn't taken the money yet. Her only crime, as far as anybody would know, would be playing hooky. She could even say, if she was discovered, that she had gone to school this morning and had felt sick and came home. That was true enough: She *did* feel sick.

She listened intently, but heard nothing else.

Maneuvering on her hands and knees, she peaked under the desk, surveying as much as she could see of the room. No pairs of feet loomed on the hardwood or worn carpet.

Silently, T.C. rose from behind the desk. She was still

alone in the room. Her mother had only closed the sliding doors.

There was nothing to stop her now. The money was inches from her hand. All she had to do was take it.

Her fingers reached up, grasped the brass handle; the deep, heavy drawer slid open. On the left side, next to a bank book and a small cardboard file in which Neil kept receipts, sat the money box: an old scratched and dented English tea tin, with a painting of the Brighton Pavilion on the lid. There was no way of locking it. It sat there, she thought, waiting for somebody to lift it out and pluck off the lid. It might as well be her as somebody else.

She stared down at the streaked onion-shaped domes of the Pavilion, at the unnatural grass and flowers painted in the foreground and the gawdy blue unlike any sky that she had ever seen, and told herself that it would teach Neil a lesson. He was too damned trusting. Nobody should be so trusting. He was a grown-up and ought to know better.

Angrily, she snatched the box out of the drawer, balanced it on a pile of typed sheets of paper, jerked off the lid, and looked down onto the neatly arranged bills inside. He had them grouped according to denomination: the five-dollar bills paper-clipped together, the tens, the twenties. The ones had a rubber band around them.

She counted ten ones and slipped them out from beneath the red rubber band. Then she slipped two tens out from under one paper clip and one twenty from beneath another paper clip.

Fifty dollars. It would have to be enough.

She set the lid back on the box, pushed it down firmly, and replaced the box. One last look at the absurd Pavilion and she closed the drawer. There. Nobody would know that she had touched the desk. Everything was exactly as she had found it.

All she had to do was make her escape.

She slipped out the front door, but as she ran around the house she glanced out the front gate and saw a frighteningly familiar car passing. Caper's mother and stepfather sat like statues in the front seat. Her stomach did a flip-flop, but the car went on past.

Were they looking for Caper? Had they made the association between his disappearance and her? Or was this a coincidence? Not taking time to stop and think, she hurled herself down the driveway to the garage.

"I'll be glad when we're out of Berkeley," she told Caper, as she crashed into the storeroom. "You don't know how glad!"

She lunged across the room and threw up in the corner. Her body heaving, she braced herself against the wall and gagged and spit up her breakfast and part of her dinner from the night before. Caper watched with an interested expression while she wiped her mouth and chin and collapsed on the old sofa.

"Why did I do it?" she moaned. "Why did I take that money?"

She felt as if she had committed a murder. And, in a sense, she had, for when Neil and the others knew that she had stolen the money their opinion of her would be murdered.

"I could put it back," she said, more to herself than to Caper. "But I won't." Stubbornly, she glared at the boy, as if *he* were the one urging her to return the fifty dollars.

The taste in her mouth was awful. She wished that she had something to drink.

5

Nobody on the BART train paid attention to the twelve-year-old girl with the backpack and tightly rolled sleeping bag or the thin younger boy with the bruised face peering out from beneath a striped stocking cap. The pair sat quietly beneath a poster of a suntanned man in a plaid shirt who proclaimed to the world that he smoked because he liked it.

Anyone who looked at them with some interest would have seen that the boy was scared and the girl was holding his hand and whispering to him in an effort to sooth him. Each time the train halted, the boy jumped and looked around, his eyes large and his fists clenched, as if he expected somebody to attack him, and the girl had to renew her efforts to calm him.

Since she didn't know where they were going, T.C. decided to get off the train at the first stop on the San Francisco side of the bay.

Clinging to the smooth black rubber railing, they let the escalator carry them up to the street level. Huge glass-walled office buildings and strangely angled concrete and glass hotel facades loomed around them. They stood close together on the wide brick sidewalk, gazing up at the distant tops of the buildings, while impatient men and women hurried past them on both sides.

T.C. felt dizzy, as if she had found herself balanced on the edge of a cliff.

Market Street stretched in one direction as far as she could see, like one of those perspective drawings in art class. Framed with a confused assortment of old and new buildings and choked with streetcars and buses, it looked like an obstacle course that she did not yet dare attempt.

Facing the other direction, the street opened into a plaza in front of an old building with a clock tower. The Ferry Building. Of course! She remembered, now: That was where people used to get on and off the ferries to cross the bay before the bridge and the tube were built.

She didn't have any idea which way to go, but at least it looked less crowded toward the Ferry Building. She adjusted the pack on her shoulders and took Caper by the hand.

Heading across the plaza, which was much bigger than the one at the university, T.C. was surprised to encounter several rows of sidewalk vendors, just like the people who sold things along Telegraph Avenue in Berkeley. Young men with long hair and beards peddled hand-tooled belts and jewelry and sand-cast candles, and young women in flowing skirts or tight jeans held up puppets and tie-dyed blouses. An artist had propped up a sign, offering to sketch portraits of passersby; some of the sample drawings around the wooden easel were pretty good, but his prettified portraits of movie stars didn't look much like the people they were supposed to represent.

The vendors frightened Caper; he held back, trying to keep his distance. Across the plaza, they discovered a great confusion of concrete boxes and massive beams jutting into the air like a collapsed building. Then T.C. saw the pool around it and the water gushing out of the beams and boxes, and realized that it was a fountain. It made Ludwig's Fountain at the university look like a bathtub.

T.C. and Caper walked all the way around the huge fountain and then sat on the edge of it. Caper dipped his hands in the foamy water and splashed some on the pavement. For the first time since leaving home, a smile appeared on his face.

T.C. looked up at the clock on the Ferry Building. It dawned on her why so many people were rushing about: It was the end of the working day. People were on their way home. Soon it would be dinnertime. Already, she was hungry. But before she and Caper could think about food, she had to find them a place to spend the night.

Where, in all of San Francisco, could two runaway kids sleep?

She had though that they could camp out, but she didn't see any likely places to spread their sleeping bag. She had heard about kids getting arrested for sleeping in parks, and she knew what would happen if she and Caper were picked up: They would be sent back to Berkeley "so fast their heads would swim," as Malvina would say.

In a movie once she had seen two people sleeping in a giant sewer pipe that was waiting to be buried, but she didn't know where she would fine one of those.

She glanced at Caper. He was still splashing water onto the pavement. *He* wasn't worried. She had to do the worrying for both of them.

"Ahhhh-yah!"

T.C. looked up. Three kids about her age were climbing on the fountain, chasing each other and shouting. She wondered how they had got so high up on those square pipes. They must have been two stories above the pavement.

"Hey, you kids! Get down from there!" A cop strode across the plaza, gesturing angrily. The kids shouted obscenities and began clambering down from the fountain. T.C. decided that she and Caper should move on, too. Taking his hand, she pulled him after her. He didn't want to leave the water, but she dragged him away. A sudden inspiration told her that they had to keep moving. As long as they were on the move nobody could hassle them, but if they stopped, if they looked as if they didn't have a place to go, they'd be in trouble.

T.C. herded the boy through the narrow canyons of the financial district, past ornate old buildings and shining new ones, all spewing out the men and women who labored all day within them. They were caught up in the crowds, bumped and jostled, sent spinning in circles, turned around, cursed, and pushed aside by tired office workers rushing to their own destinations.

"Don't worry, Caper," she said, reassuring herself as much as the boy. "We'll find a place to go."

They began to climb a hill, heading away from the skyscrapers toward neighborhoods of smaller, older buildings. They passed Chinese restaurants and shops with Chinese characters painted on the windows, and T.C. wondered if this was Chinatown, but they missed the central area of Chinatown and walked up narrow, twisting streets lined with apartment buildings and Italian cafés and coffee shops. Every time she considered resting, she saw a policeman and remembered to keep moving.

Caper dragged his feet, whimpering and whining, like a tired animal. She didn't know how much longer she could keep him going. Maybe, if they did nothing else, they should stop someplace and eat. If only she could find a hot dog stand or a McDonald's. But the restaurants they passed looked expensive, or the kind of places that wouldn't want two kids without any adults along.

She saw a man lying on the sidewalk, his head on a beer can, his dirty, naked feet dangling in the gutter, and wondered why the police didn't arrest him. But maybe they would. Maybe they hadn't noticed him yet.

She was tired, but not discouraged. She believed that something good would happen to her and Caper. She wasn't sure what, but she couldn't imagine this adventure turning out badly. Someone would help them. A nice person would offer them a place to stay, near Golden Gate Park—or the beach! That was what she wanted, to live near the Pacific Ocean, with a room of her own. This was what she craved most: a room of her own. And these people, whoever they were, would take Caper to a doctor and they'd discover that nothing was wrong with Caper's hearing. He would stop being afraid and would learn to talk, and they'd be happy together. Then she would call her parents and they would come to San Francisco and see how happy she and Caper were with these new people and would understand what had been wrong at the commune. Neil would be sorry that he hadn't let Caper be part of their family. And then . . .then T.C. and Caper would go back to Berkeley with her parents, because they *were* her parents, and she did love them, and they would have their own home, and be a normal family, the four of them, just as she had always craved.

That was her dream!

A joyful recklessness possessed her as she dragged the boy along the sidewalk; the afternoon, the city, the whole world was filled with possibilities. It was exciting to be risking the future.

The neighborhood they were wandering into reminded T.C. of Berkeley: the narrow street was lined with little bookstores and art galleries and more junk shops than she could count. She stopped several times to look through the plant-hung windows of espresso cafés and tiny restaurants but she was afraid to take Caper into any of them. He might make a scene, trip over something, call attention to them, and then they'd be in trouble.

They were crossing the street when Caper fell down. He didn't trip on the curb. He just fell.

"Caper!"

She stopped and tried to pick him up, but he was limp, lying in the street like a giant rag doll. Tugging on his arms, she dragged him to the edge of the street and pushed him up on the curb. He seemed to have no backbone. It was as if his strength had left him all at one.

He wasn't tough enough, she told herself. I shouldn't have made him walk so far.

She sat on the high granite curb and propped him up against her. The bruises and sores from the burns were dark against his washed-out face. Somewhere, he had lost the stocking cap. The raw places in his scalp oozed pus. He couldn't keep his eyes open and his breathing sounded hoarse and strained.

"Caper!" she begged. "Don't die! Please don't die!"

She unzipped the side pocket of the backpack and dug out a can of Coke that she had stolen from the commune's kitchen. Popping the top, she tried to pour some of the foamy stuff into Caper's mouth. Most of it dribbled down his chin and onto the front of his borrowed T-shirt and jacket.

"Please, Caper! We'll rest. I'll buy you something to eat, I promise!"

Grasping his head, she shook him and tried to force him to drink more of the Coke. He gagged and began coughing. The spasm started deep in his chest and shook his scrawny body, but when it had passed he looked somewhat more alert.

"Caper?"

She hoisted him to his feet and made him shuffle along the sidewalk.

All this time, not one of the passersby offered to help. Nobody even stopped. A few people glared at T.C. and Caper, but most of them pretended that they saw nothing. Maybe they actually did see nothing. Maybe they had trained themselves to be so blind to other people that they never noticed Caper sprawled in the street.

It made T.C. mad. "You could've really been dying," she told Caper, "and nobody would've cared."

He groaned and rested his head against her shoulder. At that moment, T.C. saw the Hot Dog Palace.

"It's okay, Caper. We're going to eat!"

She looked down at his face and saw that his cheeks were shiny wet from tears. It was her fault. She had intended to take care of him, and had practically killed him.

Pushing open the heavy glass door, T.C. guided Caper down the steps into the Hot Dog Palace. In a corner building shaped like a flat iron on a steep hill, the Hot Dog Palace was constructed on two levels, with a counter at one end where a pimply young man and a girl with long hair dyed an unnatural red sold hot dogs and soft drinks, and plastic-topped tables scattered every place else. The walls, floors, ceiling, and furnishings in the Hot Dog Palace were all the color of French's Prepared Mustard.

T.C. propped Caper at one of the corner tables on the upper level, and set her backpack and sleeping bag on a mustard-yellow chair before going down to the counter to buy hot dogs and root beers. On impulse, she also pondered a plastic basket of french fries.

The Hot Dog Palace was almost empty. A couple of teenagers sat chainsmoking at one ashtray-littered table, an old woman slept with her head among plastic dishes and crumpled napkins on another table, and a tiny person who might have been either a man or a woman sat mumbling into his coffee a few tables away from where T.C. had left Caper. When she carried the tray with the hot dogs, root beers, and fries back to the upper level of the Hot Dog Palace, he was still muttering at the empty plastic cup, as if trying to make it refill itself by chanting a magic spell, but unable to remember the right words.

T.C. thrust the hot dog at Caper. He stared at it for a moment, then snatched it out of her hands and shoved it into his mouth. "Not so fast! You'll choke." But it was useless, so T.C. turned her attention to her own dog.

As she chewed the leathery frankfurter and dry, tasteless bun, T.C. thought of home, the commune, of her father with a fistful of nuts and bolts and a hood ornament in his pocket, ready to expound on his latest discoveries; of her mom, drying her hands on her apron after washing the dishes, and turning around with a look of surprise on her bland features as T.C. told her for the hundredth time that she wished she had more privacy; of Neil's white beard waggling up and down as he expounded on the future of the commune and the beauty of their life of sharing; and of the boys in the backyard, shouting and passing the basketball between them and leaping toward the hoop nailed onto the side of the house.

Surely, by now, they must be wondering where she was. What were they thinking? Did any of them, except her parents, of course, care if she was there, or not? Even her mother and father; how much would her absence change their lives? Not much, she was willing to bet.

She felt homesick, but her resolve strengthened as she remembered how Neil had refused to help her to save Caper. Twice. That was what she resented most of all. Neil had been afraid, too cowardly to risk his precious commune by saving this miserable kid.

She slouched at the yellow plastic-topped table, washing down her hot dog and French fries with root beer and feeling mauled by the endless procession of memories and fears that assailed her.

When she reached across the table for a paper napkin from the dispenser, she noticed that the little person with the coffee mug was watching her. She pretended that she hadn't seen him and wiped the catsup from her chin, but he continued staring at her with his nasty little eyes. She wondered if he might be a plainclothes cop, like the ones she had seen on TV. She finished off her second hot dog and was eager to leave, but Caper pulled on her sleeve and opened his mouth like a baby bird to show that he was still hungry.

"Okay," she said. "I'll get you some ice cream."

She bought a pair of ice cream sandwiches. On the way back to her table, she was careful not to look at the little person, but she knew that he was staring at her.

That bright, almost empty Hot Dog Palace was scary now, with its glossy mustard-yellow tables on which the remains of meals and snacks were scattered like the aftermath of a storm, and that person staring, staring, staring. T.C. might have fallen into one of those science fiction movies in which people's bodies are possessed by demons or creatures from outer space, turning them into blank-eyed zombies. But she wouldn't let that jerk know that she was scared. He probably got his thrills frightening kids, and she wasn't going to give him the satisfaction of seeing her react.

T.C. peeled the wrapping from one of the ice cream sandwiches. Out of the corner of her eye, she saw the creep was still watching them. Pretending indifference, she peeled back the paper on her ice cream sandwich and took a bite.

The next thing she knew, the little person was standing beside the table, his mustard-spotted chest six inches from her elbow.

"How long you been run away?"

"Huh?"

"How long you run away from home? A week? Two days? How long?"

The person looked like an ugly little doll. He wasn't much taller than Caper, but a lot fatter, with a squished nose and ears like two question marks facing each other.

T.C. glared at him. He was just a pile of dandruff. "I'm not afraid of you."

He smirked at her, his mouth wide like a frog's. " 'Course not. I ain't nobody to be scared of." He leaned forward confidentially, smelling of onions. "You just run away t'day?" T.C. refused to reply, but he persisted: "Ya got a place to crash?"

He smiled and, for an instant, long enough to catch T.C. off guard, he lost that insane look in his small clenched eyes.

She shook her head.

Caper made a noise and they both turned to watch him

finish his ice cream. His face, hands, and clothes were all smeared with food.

"I know a place where you and your brother can sleep tonight. And it don't cost nothing."

T.C. pretended to be unimpressed by this announcement.

Silent waves of intuition rushed through her brain and she knew that in some scary way this little man was going to be important to her and Caper. She didn't want any part of him, but she felt as if she had no choice. That they were brought together at this time, in this place, seemed like . . . like fate.

T.C.'s thoughts were interrupted by the sound of high-heeled boots on the composition tile floor, as a woman in tight jeans, a pink T-shirt with the words "Sweet Dreams" sprawled across her breasts in gold glitter letters, and a fringed, over-the-shoulder cloth bag swaying against one hip, strolled into the Hot Dog Palace. The little man jumped around and, a grin distorting his homely features, waved at the woman.

"Hi, sugar!" he called, "how's it goin' tonight?"

The woman, whom T.C. saw wasn't as young as she at first appeared, looked surprised, and then shrugged her shoulders. Before the doll-like person standing beside T.C.'s table could say anything else, she sashayed over to the order counter.

"Friend o' mine," the little person told T.C. "She'll tell you: You can count on me. I'm one hunnerd percent trustworthy."

T.C. nodded, but the little man didn't seem to be satisfied with her response.

"I got lots of friends—you'd be surprised how many friends I got—and they'd all tell you, ever' one of 'em, how honest I am. Ever'body likes me. I can go any damn place in this city and find people who call me by name and wave to me and ask how I am. Just like that girl, there. I always say, if a person is popular, he don't need nothing else. And that's one thing I sure am: popular."

T.C. tried to look impressed, but another question was bothering her. "How'd you know about us?" she asked. "That we were runaways?"

He grinned. "I picked up the vibes, know what I mean?"

T.C. didn't like this person, but she didn't know what else she and Caper were going to do. "What kind of place is it? Where we can stay?"

He grinned again: "Where I live, sweetheart. Nice. Not fancy, but nice. Come on. It ain't far. Your brother, he looks done in."

T.C. nodded. The brief spurt of energy the food had given Caper had faded, and he was slumped in his chair, his scarred head resting on his arms. He looked like a baby sleeping. She had to think of him. Taking care of somebody else limited her choices. She couldn't afford to be too damned picky.

She glanced at the little man again, wondering what his game was. Why did he want to help them? While she was looking at him, she realized whom he resembled, more than anybody else in the world: Mickey Mouse. What he ought to do, she thought, was go to Disneyland and get a job playing Mickey Mouse.

"Maybe," she said. "Just tonight. Until we find someplace to stay." Then, grudgingly: "It's nice of you to offer."

He gestured expansively with his stubby arms: "My pleasure, sweetheart. Name is Aldiss. What should I call you? Just first names. I don't want to know nothing else about you. Don't want you to worry I'm gonna turn you in, or nothin'."

It didn't occur to T.C. to give false names. "He's Caper.

I'm T.C." She couldn't bring herself to quite look Aldiss in the face, so she glanced past him at the woman in the pink shirt leaning over the counter across the room, flirting with the pimply young guy cramming her purchases into a paper bag. T.C. wondered if she was trying to get him to charge her less or give her free fries, or something like that. Even from where T.C. sat, the clerk looked embarrassed.

"Okay, T.C.," said the little man. "Wake him up, and let's go!"

T.C. rousted Caper, and, unwillingly, he pulled himself upright. Aldiss stared at the bruises and burns on the boy's face and hands. He raised his eyebrows when he got to the big wound in Caper's scalp.

"Your parents, huh?" T.C. started to say something, but Aldiss kept on talking. "I'll tell you somethin', girl. Lots of kids run away 'cause their old man or old lady beat up on 'em. San Francisco's filled with runaway kids whose parents used 'em for punchin' bags. No kiddin', I know for a *fact*, there're hunnerds of kids who been beat up by their parents right in this city."

Let him think what he wants, T.C. decided. It doesn't hurt me.

She maneuvered Caper up the steps out of the Hot Dog Palace. For a little guy, Aldiss walked pretty fast. It wasn't easy for T.C. and Caper to keep up with him as he limped along the narrow sidewalk, forcing his way among the evening crowds.

Krishna devotees with saffron robes and shaved heads ambled near, waving sticks of incense and shaking jingle bells. T.C. jumped out of the way when a couple of guys in black leather costumes strode past, but they didn't seem to notice her existence. Rock music blasted out of a coffee shop, and down the street an aria from an Italian opera rolled through the open doors of an espresso place mingling with the pungent aroma of fresh-ground, brewing coffee.

Aldiss turned abruptly, staring in the direction of T.C. and Caper; the light from a streetlamp caught his dark glasses and made them shine like two disks of black obsidian, giving the impression that his eye sockets were vacant. He tossed his cigarette in a fast, sparkling arc into the night and resumed his quick, steady limp up the hill.

I'm not afraid, T.C. told herself, squeezing Caper's bony hand. Everything is going to be okay. I'm not afraid.

How could you tell about people? That was the hardest thing in life. All you could go by was how they looked and what they said. It wasn't fair to judge someone because he was ugly, and you couldn't go around calling everybody a liar. No, you took your chances and prayed that you didn't goof up.

They headed up a street narrower and steeper than the one they had been climbing; the street pavement was corrugated to give the tires on the cars better traction, but the broken sidewalk was hard to walk on. The aging apartment houses cowered behind overflowing garbage cans and cardboard cartons. Skinny cats strolled beneath the streetlamps, hunting for their dinners.

T.C. pointed out the cats to Caper, but he was too far gone to appreciate them. A sleepwalker, he responded only to her steering.

Aldiss looked back again, tossing them a brutal little smile. He stopped in front of a three-story brown building with two rows of broken Spanish tiles raised like eyebrows above a pair of bay window eyes and paint blistering like a bad case of acne. T.C. caught up with him. They were eyeball to eyeball. A mustache of moistness glittered on his upper lip. Webs of wrinkles sprouted like patterns of erosion from beneath his dark glasses. He was a lot older than she had thought; she wouldn't have been surprised if he was older than her parents.

"Second floor," he said, "I better go first. Bastard landlord's too cheap to put light bulbs in the hall."

Panic slammed into T.C.'s stomach like something ice cold that she had swallowed. Was she really going to take Caper into that building with this crazy man she knew nothing about? But she couldn't think of a way to get out of it. They had gone too far to retreat.

A square of cardboard was taped over one broken window pane on the door, which opened on a flight of the steepest, darkest stairs T.C. had ever seen. Two other doors apparently led to apartments on the lower floor. Aldiss huffed and puffed up the stairs and T.C. shifted the weight of her backpack and grasped Caper by the arm.

The second-floor hallway smelled as if somebody had gone to the bathroom in it. T.C. suspected that cats had been sick there, too.

Aldiss pulled out a key and unfastened the padlock on his door. T.C. had never seen a padlock used on an apartment or house door. He flicked on a light and kicked aside some clothes scattered on the entry floor.

"Drop your things anywhere."

When he flashed that babydoll smile again, T.C. noticed how tiny his teeth were. They were so even and white that she decided they must be fake.

"Can I use your bathroom?" she asked him.

"Sure!" He pointed to a door. "Don't you want to leave your backpack out here?"

"I need something in it."

It wasn't easy to maneuver in the narrow bathroom, but she slid the bolt and took off the backpack and dug out the money she had brought with her. After using the toilet (that was a relief—she'd been afraid all day to leave Caper long enough to go into a ladies' room!) she stuffed her money into her underwear.

When she came out of the bathroom, she discovered Caper in his underwear asleep on a bare mattress on the floor, the wounds on his arms and legs clearly visible, even in the dim light. His clothes were in a heap nearby.

"I helped him," said Aldiss.

"Thanks."

T.C. unrolled the sleeping bag. The damp walls seemed as soft as pillows, ready to collapse and smother them as they slept. Another stained mattress lay on the floor a little distance away, next to an old kitchen table and a couple of kitchen chairs. Nearby were some cardboard boxes heaped with clothes and an orange crate with a clock, a radio, and a crookneck lamp arranged on it. Aldiss was either just moving in or about to move out.

"Want something to drink?" he asked. "I got beer in the fridge. Maybe a Pepsi."

He pointed to a half-open louvered door that she hadn't noticed and the cluttered kitchenette beyond it. She shook her head.

"Too tired."

Visions of drugged soda pop danced through her head. She was sure that it was stupid, but she couldn't shake the idea. Anyway, she was bushed.

Squatting on the mattress beside Caper, she pulled off her shoes. It felt good to get them off.

"Look, uh . . . Aldiss, thanks. I mean, it was nice of you to let us stay here. I appreciate it."

The little man danced around her, grinning and waving his pintsized arms.

"Think nothing of it. I *like* to help people, especially *young* people, know what I mean? Relax, okay? Get a good night's sleep. Like somebody said, tomorrow's another goddamn day."

T.C. nodded and crawled into the sleeping bag beside Caper. She did not take off her clothes.

It was good to stretch out in the sleeping bag, even on that lumpy, cigarette-stinking mattress. She was more exhausted than she had let herself admit. But she had succeeded, had taken care of herself and Caper, got them through their first day.

This was how she would do it: one day at a time. It was the best way. Mustn't worry . . . everything . . . okay. . .

Her eyes were closed and she was almost asleep when she became aware of the sound of a voice droning on and on someplace above her. "That's right, sleep. You'll be okay here. You can trust me . . . I'll take care of you. . . ."

What was he saying? She opened her eyes and peered up at the squat figure swaying beside the mattress, grinning like some kind of hyena and gesturing with a can of beer wedged so firmly into one fist that it looked as if it had grown there.

". . . Friends . . . My friends know what I'm like. They ain't hoodlums or creeps, not *my* friends. I got real influential people for friends, you'd be surprised. I'm telling you the truth. You can believe every word."

What was he babbling about? She couldn't make sense out of it, but he kept on talking and talking, as if he were trying to convince her of something important before it was too late.

Crazy, she thought. He must be crazy.

"I want you to meet my friends, T.C. Tomorrow, I'm gonna introduce you to my friends. You'll be so impressed, I know you will."

He was crazy, but she couldn't keep her eyes open. Her eyelids were too heavy, as heavy as the rest of her body, which was sinking into the mattress, sinking right through the floor, into the blackness that was swirling around her. The droning of his voice was part of the blackness, part of a dream that rose like a spider web from the darkness and enveloped her.

The battle was lost, and the security of sleep enfolded her. Until. . . .

She never did understand why she woke up at the exact moment when she did. Maybe she had ESP. But the next thing she knew she was awake and listening to a shuffling near her. It sounded like an animal rooting around. Then she heard a zipper and knew that the animal was going through her backpack.

Cautiously, she opened her eyes and saw Aldiss bent over the backpack, pawing through it.

Well, let him. There was nothing in it but clothes. Her Swiss army knife and money were in her underwear, pressing against her stomach. That jerk wasn't as smart as he thought he was.

She was both disappointed in him—she had wanted to believe that he was a friend—and mad at herself. She should've known better than to expect anything else from an adult.

She wouldn't trust anybody, but she especially wouldn't trust grown-ups. This thought lingering in her head, she slipped again into the soft blackness of sleep.

The knife cut into her flesh, pierced her ribs, penetrated to her organs. . . .

She woke up, twisted around, then realized that the pain in her side was caused by the sharp, bony elbow of Caper. Gently, she shifted him, edging away in the confines of the sleeping bag. Greenish, sickly light poured through the tall naked windows. The shredded windowshades had been rolled up and the morning revealed the filth of the apartment.

Pulling herself upright, T.C. surveyed the stark ugliness around her. The only objects that could have been called decorative were the dusty wine bottles arranged on a windowsill ledge. Except for water stains, the walls were bare. There wasn't even an old calendar.

She heard a crash and turned in time to see Aldiss stamping his tiny foot in rage. He had dropped a jar of instant coffee on the kitchenette floor. The dark-brown powder was scattered from the greasy patch of linoleum into the room in which T.C. and Caper lay.

"*Shit*!"

Then Aldiss saw that he had an audience. The petulant creases on each side of his mouth were shoved into dimples and he offered T.C. a rueful smile.

"We'll have to do without coffee this A.M.," he said. "In fact, sweetheart, we'll have to do without breakfast altogether. There ain't another thing to eat in the house."

"That doesn't matter." T.C. crawled out of the sleeping bag and groped for her shoes.

"I don't even got the wherewithall to buy us breakfast." Aldiss's stubby arms gestured tragically. "It breaks my heart to say it, because there ain't nothin' I like better'n treatin' my friends to real elegant, sit-down feed. I want you to know, if I had a single crust of French toast, it would be yours!"

Aldiss stared at T.C., but she pretended that she didn't understand what he was trying to hint at.

"We'd better be going, anyway," she said. "Thanks for letting us sleep on your mattress."

She woke up Caper and helped him into his clothes. The bruises and welts on his back were still painful; one massive bruise ranged spectacularly in color from yellow-green to blue-purple.

"There's a doughnut shop on the corner," Aldiss said.

"Yeah?"

T.C. tied Caper's shoes for him and helped him on with his jacket.

"Hey, listen, friends," said Aldiss. "I tell you what: I ain't got no food, but I got something better. How about a little pot for breakfast?"

"Huh?" Was he kidding her? "You mean dope? Like in the movies?"

Aldiss shook his lumpy head. "Forget it. I was spoofin'."

T.C. zipped up her coat. Jack had bragged about using pot, and some of the adults in the commune had tried it. She didn't think her parents had, but Neil probably had. He believed in "consciousness expansion." She had never bothered with dope, and wasn't particularly interested in it. She wasn't going to let anybody push that stuff onto Caper. In his condition, who could tell what it might do to him?

"Give me some coins, girlie, and I'll go pick us up some doughnuts. I know you've got money."

T.C. shook her head. "No, honest. Caper and me, we don't have any money."

She pulled the sleeping bag straight and began to roll it up. All she wanted was to get Caper and herself out of this guy's crummy place before he did something crazy. He might try to beat her up. She had been stupid before, but this was like she was trying to set a record for dumbness. Coming up here was, without a doubt, the lame-brainest thing she had ever done.

"You expect me to believe that, sweetheart?"

T.C. tied up the sleeping bag and stuffed it into the place reserved for it on the backpack.

"You're a lying little bitch."

The diminutive man was twitching and jerking like a spastic idiot, waggling a pudgy forefinger at her.

"You tricked me," he shouted. "I thought you had money. I saw you buy hot dogs and ice cream. I saw you. You gotta have money."

T.C. hoisted the backpack onto her shoulders. "That was the last. I don't have anything else. Some pennies, that's all. I gotta go find my uncle. I have an uncle in San Francisco. I'm supposed to go see him. Today. This morning. He's expecting me—us."

"Bullshit."

T.C. took Caper's hand. "Come on, Caper. We gotta go." She led the boy to the door, but didn't take her eyes off Aldiss. "Thanks a lot, mister. We appreciate it."

The little man's face glowed red until he looked as if he were going to have a fit. He darted across the room, wedging himself between T.C. and the door.

"No, you don't! You ain't gettin' out o' here so damned easy." He plopped his fat hand on the backpack. "I'm your friend. Friends help each other, right? I helped you. Now, you gotta help me."

That sickening smile again: The cruelty beneath it glittered like the teeth of a shark.

"*Me . . . me . . . me!*"

The guy was nuts! T.C. could smell his foul breath, count the pores on his stubby nose, the veins throbbing in his forehead.

"Let me go! I've got to see my uncle. He'll get the police out looking for me if I'm not there soon." She almost believed that she did have an uncle in San Francisco.

Suddenly, Caper parted his lips and let out a howl. He sounded like a wounded dog. The cry could be heard all over the building. It grew, rising in intensity, his mouth opening wider and wider until he filled the morning with his bellow.

"All right, all right!" The little man covered his ears. "Get the hell out of here. But don't let me set eyes on either one of you again. Shut him up and get out of here!"

He pushed them out of the door and slammed it after them. T.C. grabbed Caper's hand and dragged him down the steep stairs. She slipped on some garbage and nearly fell half the length of the stairwell, but her hand flew out against the damp wall and she regained her balance. They clattered past the door with the broken window and into the street. Running down the block, they turned the corner and made their way down one street after another, twisting and turning until they reached Grant Avenue.

Their chests heaved, their lungs burned, as the cold morning air rushed in and out. Caper fell and skinned his hand on the rough pavement and cried as they ran.

They passed the Hot Dog Palace, but it was closed. In Chinatown, they stopped at a coffee shop and had Danish pastries and hot chocolate for breakfast. T.C. had to go into the rest room to fish the money out of her underwear to pay the bill.

6

That morning, T.C. did some serious thinking. She had to find a way to make money. It wouldn't take long for the fifty dollars, and her own twenty, to evaporate. She thought about the vendors in Berkeley on Telegraph Avenue and the ones at the plaza by the Ferry Building, and wondered if she could make or sell something in order to support herself and Caper.

She had never had to think about earning money before, not so that she could eat and have a roof over her head. Of course, she had "earned" money at home so that she could buy presents for people on their birthdays and at Christmas, but that was playacting and this was real life.

She realized after only one night away from home how much she had been protected, how much her parents and the others had taken care of her.

And what, she wondered, was happening across the bay, in Berkeley? Were they upset, crying, scared that she was dead? How long would it be until they accepted the fact that she was gone? Did she want them to forget her?

Part of her said yes, but another part of her liked the idea of them suffering. They had never appreciated her; maybe now, when it was too late, they'd realize the value of the girl they had had among them.

And what about Caper's parents? Did they miss their punching bag? Were they searching for him, or were they glad to be rid of him?

As T.C. and Caper left the Chinese coffee shop, they passed a huge construction of pastries and cookies. Glazed or powdered with sugar and decorated with chopped and slivered nuts and candied cherries and bits of peach or apricot or strawberry preserves, the confections rose in neat, glorious layers: a mountain of temptation.

Caper stopped, staring at the bounty, and, with wonder in his eyes, put out a hand. T.C. slapped his fingers before they could make contact with one of the sugar-coated beauties.

Caper turned and stared at T.C. with baffled rage. It was the first time that she had struck him. He didn't understand, and it angered him. His little, bony hands closed into fists and his face twisted into a mask of inarticulate fury. He wanted to hurt her, too. She was like the others. If she could hit him, then what else would she do? She saw it all pass over his features, and she felt ashamed and angry with herself.

I mustn't ever do it again, she told herself. Whatever he does, I'm not going to hit him.

She took his face in her hands and made him look at her. "I'm sorry, Caper. Can you understand that? I'm sorry. But you can't have any cookies. We have to save our money until I get a job." She spoke slowly, carefully, trying harder than she ever had before to make him comprehend both her words and her tone of voice. "Caper? Do you understand what I'm saying?"

He jerked free from her grip. He was still sulking, but it was more an act of willful independence than of anger. She took his hand and led him out of the store and up the narrow, crowded sidewalk.

They hesitated at open fish markets to look at strange, brightly colored creatures of the deep. It was hard to believe that people ate those pink and blue and silver monsters, with their bulbous eyes and spiny fins and wide, snaggle-toothed smiles. They paused at a produce market, admiring the fresh beauty of the stacks of carrots and onions and greens, and the gaudy colors and unusual shapes of unfamiliar vegetables. Shrill Chinese music followed them down the block.

They strolled the length of Grant Avenue, staring into store windows, eyeing the vast quantities of souvenirs waiting to catch the fancy of the tourists. T.C. was fascinated by the workmanship of the carved ivory and admired the painted fans and beautifully dressed dolls. She didn't care about owning any of those things, but they were interesting to look at.

Roast ducks and stuffed chickens dangled from cords behind delicatessen windows; brocade jackets and beaded satin dresses hung in open doorways, watched by wrinkled Chinese ladies sitting on tall stools behind the counters. Electric fans sent bursts of spicy aromas out of restaurants and grocery stores, and tourists trudged up the hill munching on fortune cookies and meat-stuffed dumplings.

We're not tourists, T.C. reminded herself. We can't spend a few days here and then go home. We have to find a way to live.

In a hillside park, T.C. let Caper play on the swings and monkey bars. After a short time, he flopped on the grass, and she had an opportunity to think about their situation.

Things weren't working out as she had expected. She realized now that she had made no plans. She had come here with Caper trusting to chance, but that wasn't good enough.

An old man shuffled past, dragging a gunnysack over the pavement behind him. She watched as he stomped a beer can lying on the edge of the grass and dropped it into his sack. A few paces farther he found another can, flattened it, and added it to his collection. His movements were painfully slow and deliberate. He looked as if he must be a hundred years old. How much money would he get for those cans? Was it worth the time and effort?

Her thoughts were distracted by an Indian war cry. A trio of blond children ran into the park, followed by a thin young woman in a plain brown cloth coat. They wore spotless pastel clothes, shiny new shoes, and carried brightly colored balls and toys. T.C. thought that she never had seen such attractive children. She looked down at her own grubby, slept-in clothes, and realized what she and Caper must look like beside those three blond angels. She glanced over at Caper and was startled by the expression on his face. He was staring at those kids as if they were made of sugar and he were starving to death.

"Come on," T.C. told him. "We'll be all right." She collected Caper and they hiked down the hills toward the busy center of the city.

She couldn't stop hoping that something would turn up. Even their encounter with that bastard Aldiss hadn't cured her of her blind belief that they would be okay.

They rested at Union Square, watching tourists taking snapshots of each other with the gray hulk of the St. Francis Hotel in the background. They saw old men and young bums in gray T-shirts and ragged trousers and shoes with no soles sleeping on newspapers spread on the grass or on green-painted benches. T.C. watched young people in leather jackets and Levis laughing and shouting as they passed open beer cans back and forth. She stared with fascination at elegantly dressed men and women striding through the square, heads high, as if unaware of the disreputable types lounging around them. The contrast between the dirty, shabby people who seemed to have no place to go and the well-dressed ones who had destinations was frightening.

You have to have a place to go. That's the difference between the bums and the others. T.C. and Caper had no place to go.

She and Caper trudged down the hill, past crowded souvenir shops and porno movie theaters, until they reached Market Street. At first, T.C. didn't understand what the mob of people crowded at the end of Powell was doing, and then she realized that they all were waiting to ride a clanging cable car to the top of Nob Hill.

She took Caper across Market Street into an old neighborhood, past crumbling buildings. They wandered past empty lots, entire blocks behind wire storm fencing in which only rubble lay, the debris left from the buildings that had been torn down to make way for urban renewal. The area looked like old photographs of cities bombed in wars. Caper and T.C. stopped and peered through the fences at piles of bricks and the remaining fragments of old walls. Occasionally, a single narrow building rose like a ghost in the center of an otherwise empty block, a temporary survivor waiting for its eventual destruction.

Looking down into the exposed basements of the now vanished buildings, T.C. and Caper watched half-wild cats prowling in and out of the rubble and glimpsed a few old men digging among the bricks and hunks of concrete as if they were looking for buried treasure. The bulldozers had left networks of shallow caves under the jagged concrete overhang of the sidewalks and streets.

Someday, huge new buildings would rise in these empty lots, replacing the slums that had been crushed and hauled away, but until construction started on the new projects the gaping holes and half-secret caves amid the rubble remained, like the ruins of an ancient city.

"Look, Caper! There goes another cat!" She pointed to the black and orange tom darting from one heap of bricks to another, perhaps in pursuit of a rodent dinner.

Pigeons, too, hunted among the ruins, swooping down to peck on the piles of rubbish and then taking off with a furious flapping of wings. The boy looked where T.C. pointed, but his expression did not betray much in the way of emotion.

A teenage boy crawled out of one of the man-made caves that once had been part of a basement and picked his way through the bricks and shattered hunks of concrete, moving like an old hand at navigating the complicated route through the excavations.

He vanished behind the ruin of a pseudo-Gothic window frame thrust up among the bricks like the eye of a needle waiting to be threaded with a shaft of sunlight, and then reappeared. Beneath his layer of dirt, he wasn't more than a couple of years older than T.C. His clothes consisted of two pairs of ragged, filthy jeans, one worn over the other to compensate for the parts lacking in each pair, half-shredded boots, and several sweatshirts and jackets pulled on, wrapped around, and hung over various sections of his anatomy. His hair stood out in greasy brown clumps from his head, except where the remains of a knit cap was scrunched down amid the tangle. His face was dark from both sunburn and ingrained dirt.

He stopped and stared at T.C. and Caper, then waved. Caper grinned and waved, too.

T.C. pulled down Caper's hand. After their experience with Aldiss, she intended to be careful whom they got mixed up with, and that filthy kid down in the rubble looked more disreputable than any hippie she had seen around Berkeley.

She tried to lead Caper away, but he broke loose and returned to the fence.

"Caper!"

He shook his head and clutched at the wire mesh with both hands.

"Caper, please!"

T.C. felt exposed, standing on the sidewalk in the center of this area of leveled blocks, with only the storm fencing rising above the street level. The sun glinted off the windows of nearby skyscrapers, like spotlights shining on the naked earth and the broken remains of the bulldozed buildings.

She wanted to run, but Caper clung to the fence as if he believed it gave him security and watched the teenage boy climbing over the rubble below.

The grimy adolescent paused and looked up, shielding his eyes with a filthy hand, and then waved again. Caper pumped his arm wildly up and down.

"Caper!" cried T.C., but he ignored her so totally that she might not have been there.

The young man maneuvered across the stark landscape like a refugee making his way across a bombed city. "Hi!"

T.C. didn't answer the call, but Caper again pumped his arm up and down.

The boy clambered across a steep pile of bricks and concrete, climbing up to the street level. "Hey!"

T.C. heard bricks falling as the boy scampered over the top of a small mountain of rubble. Suddenly he appeared on the other side of the fence. With a deft movement, he ducked down a crawled through a hole in the fence that T.C. hadn't noticed. In an instant, he stood beside them, smearing the dirt on his sweaty face with the back of his hand. "Howdy!"

T.C. took an involuntary step backward. He reeked of sweat and other unknown odors.

Caper stared at the boy, his face bright with either admiration or wonder. T.C. couldn't figure out what it was about this vagabond that appealed to Caper.

"You lookin' for a place to crash?" T.C. shrugged her shoulders.

He nodded at Caper: "That your brother? What's wrong with him? He's kinda simple, ain't he? I knew somebody was feebleminded, once. A girl. Her parents put her away so's she wouldn't have a mess of babies."

"He's not feebleminded. He just can't talk."

"Deaf an' dumb, huh? Too bad. What's your name?"

T.C. couldn't think fast enough to invent a lie. "I'm T.C.," she said. "He's Caper."

"Tee See? What does that mean?"

"They're my initials, stupid."

"Far out. My name's Goff. I live down there." He nodded toward the brick and concrete caves extending back under the sidewalk.

"Down *there*?"

"Sure. Lots of us do. Some folks been down there for months. Most people come and go, like for a few days or a week, but one old guy, *he* says he's been down there three years. Me, I've been crashin' about a month. I'm from San Jose."

"We're from . . . uh, Los Angeles."

"L.A.? I been down there. What part you from?"

"Oh, you know, in the middle. By the ocean."

The boy winked and nodded his head. "Gotcha." He tugged at the outer layer of trousers, which were so caked with filth that they were almost stiff enough to stand up by themselves. "How old're you?"

"Twelve," said T.C. "He's nine."

Goff shook his head. "You should always say you're eighteen. See, under eighteen you can get picked up, put in juvie or sent back where you come from. Me, I'm fourteen, but I always say I'm eighteen."

T.C. smiled. "Nobody would believe I'm eighteen."

"Don't make no difference. You *say* it. Most folks don't give a damn how old ya are or who ya are. They'll go along with the gag. The main idea, see, is ya gotta act like you know the ropes."

T.C. straightened her back and stared into the boy's faded blue eyes. "How do you know I'm afraid of being picked up? I didn't say I'd run away."

"Ya didn't need to. I woulda had to be blind not to see that you and him was runaways."

"How could you tell?"

He shrugged. "Just could, that's all. You know what your trouble is? I'll tell ya: You ain't got any street smarts yet."

"What?"

"You don't know how to live on the street, see? You don't got experience. You gotta learn what's what. Pick up some street smarts. Don't worry, you'll get it. I can tell you ain't so dumb. And I'll help you. Ain't hardly nothing I don't know."

T.C. took another step backward. She wasn't sure that she wanted this kid teaching her anything. He came on strong, but she didn't trust him. Not yet, anyway.

She stared down into the hole where he said he lived. She couldn't imagine living down in that mess, like a half-wild cat. She didn't want to have anything to do with that sort of life. She wondered if Goff ever took a bath. He didn't look or smell as if he did. It would be better to spread out the sleeping bag in Golden Gate Park, if she could find it, than to crawl around down there.

"You don't want to go sleeping in no parks," said the boy, as if he had read her mind. "The cops'll pick you up. They sweep through the parks every night. If they don't get you, the hoods will."

"The hoods?"

"Sure, dudes who go around looking for people to rip off. They find you, man, they'll take everything you got. I mean everything. You'll be lucky if they don't cut your throat while they're at it."

T.C. didn't know whether or not to believe him. He could be lying to get her to go down there with him so he could beat her up and rob her. He didn't seem like that kind of person, but she was lousy at figuring out people. Her mistake about Aldiss, or whatever his real name was, proved that.

Whatever anybody did to her, she couldn't go to the police, not if she didn't want to be sent home. There was nothing that she and Caper could do that was guaranteed safe. She had to choose the least scary of the options open to her.

Goff was still preaching about the gangs who roamed through the parks at night mugging people, even killing them. "Me, I never go into a park alone at night, and I ain't no chicken, either. I just don't want my brains smashed all over a tree trunk." He grinned and she saw that one of his yellowish teeth was broken off.

"Caper and I have to go see our uncle. He lives in San Francisco. We're not running away."

The boy's broken-tooth grin twisted sideways. "Who ya think you're kiddin'?"

He leaned forward, as if about to whisper a secret, and slapped his dirty paw on her shoulder. "Look, T.C., why don't you and him come on down and see my pad? It ain't so awful, and it's a lot safer'n a lot of places in this town."

"I'm not afraid."

"Then you're dumber than ya look. You gotta watch out for the cops in this town. They've declared war on us kids. Because of all the purse-snatching."

"Purse-snatching?"

"Sure, and wallet-lifting, too. See, the kids mostly pick on old folks, who can't fight back or nothing. Me, I think that's pretty crummy, but some of those kids knock the old women down so hard they break their backs or crack open their heads. The kids don't care. Let the old farts die, they say, they're cluttering up the world. The smart ones just take cash, see, because it can't be traced. But them old people don't have credit cards or nothing, anyway. Some of 'em, they're starving to death. What the kids do is wait until the old fools cash their welfare checks and get 'em on the way home from the bank."

"That's awful!"

"You think that's bad? That ain't half of what goes on in this town. I could tell you stories! I know kids no older'n him, there, who've killed old men and old women right in their rooms."

"I don't believe it."

"Why should I lie? I'm tryin' to wise you up, T.C. You got

to know what's happening if you ain't gonna get your ass wiped out. It ain't nothing to stumble on some old woman who got herself kicked to death because she wouldn't let go of her purse, or some old guy who tried to fight back when a kid grabbed his wallet. Don't matter if they only get a few bucks—those kids're mean. Listen, T.C., you have to keep your eyes open, watch people, know where they are around you, what they're doing, what they're gonna do next. Me, I'm like a cat, always ready to jump. Nobody's gonna get me."

"But stealing, beating up old people, all that . . . it's horrible."

"Hey, don't be dumb. I don't go around mugging old folks. I got my own rules. I don't hurt individuals, see? But I figure shoplifting and stuff like that is different, because the stores can afford it."

T.C. wasn't too impressed by that confession.

"There're kids who live in the cheap movies on Market, too. Just stay in 'em all night. Sometimes, they don't come out from week to week, just living on what they buy at the candy counter. You know how they pick up money? Out of the pockets of the folks who go to see the movies. A dark theater's a pretty good place to pick pockets. Sometimes, though, they hit people on the head in the johns. That's something else, T.C. You gotta be careful about public restrooms. They can be pretty dangerous places."

"I think you're making all that up to impress me."

The boy shook his head. "No, stupid. To educate you."

"What do you care about us? We're nothing to you."

"Yeah, I know that. But I like you. And I feel sorry for you. I can feel sorry for somebody, can't I?"

"What's in it for you? I mean, if we camp out down there?"

"I don't know. Maybe if I help you, you'll share your stuff

with me. Like if you got some food, or something. That'd be fair, wouldn't it? I wouldn't force you, or nothing, but if you wanted to give me something, I sure wouldn't say no."

He flashed his snaggle-toothed grin. In spite of everything, T.C. couldn't help thinking that the kid was, in his own way, honest.

She didn't want to like him, but she thought that maybe she did . . . a little.

"Hey, here comes a cop car! Come on!"

Before she realized what was happening, she and Caper were crawling behind Goff through the hole in the fence and darting down among the rubble.

"Get down, or he'll see you!"

They ducked lower, behind the piles of bricks and hunks of broken concrete, waiting for the police car to pass by.

Crouching, they moved from one small mountain of rubble to another, until they reached shallow caves under the jagged concrete overhang beneath the sidewalk and street. T.C. and Caper followed Goff behind a partition of cardboard sheets wedged into a foundation of loosely piled bricks. The cardboard made a lousy wall, if that was what it was supposed to be.

T.C. was surprised to discover that the space behind the piles of bricks and cardboard almost looked like a real room. On three sides pieces of brick walls were left over from the foundations of the buildings that had been torn down, and a partial ceiling existed where the "room" continued beneath the sidewalk. She hadn't realized that the foundations of buildings stretched under the sidewalks and streets. She had thought that they dropped straight down.

A rusty grocery store shopping car with one wheel missing stood in the middle of the cavelike room, filled with hunks of wood, newspapers and magazines, rolls of toilet paper, and a hairless celluloid doll. A heap of rags in the corner looked as if somebody might use it for a bed. A circle of charred bricks surrounded a hole in the ground where the remains of a fire, or of many fires, lay. Ragged clothing, broken pieces of furniture, cardboard cartons, and other debris were scattered over the dirt. This was somebody's home, all right, even if the wind and the rain could blow in from the open side.

It was like a stage set, thought T.C. Only there was no audience to watch the scene. Maybe she was the audience. At least, she didn't think she was part of the play.

T.C. hesitated. It occurred to her that somebody could be waiting inside. She hadn't brought Caper here to let anybody beat him up. The sense of responsibility she had acquired since knowing Caper meant a lot to her. It made her feel like a human being instead of just a kid, and it told her that she had to think before she acted, instead of plunging heedlessly forward, as she might once have done.

"Hey, come on!" Goff waved impatiently, but T.C. shook her head.

"I can see from here."

"What're ya scared of? I ain't gonna hurt ya."

The more he protested, the more certain she was that a hand with a club or a knife waited in the shadows.

Grasping Caper by the hand, she stumbled backward over the uneven mounds of bricks. Goff turned and waved his arm at her.

"Where you goin'?"

T.C. pointed to the open space beyond the cardboard partition, took a step forward, plunged nearly to the knee into a hole between piles of bricks, and toppled onto her face. Pain rushed from her ankle to her brain. Caper's hand jerked loose from hers, and he let out a wail.

Goff shouted at her, she wasn't sure what, and then Caper began tugging on her arm. The more he pulled, the more her leg, wedged between fragments of brick wall, hurt.

"Stop it!" she cried, trying to shake off Caper's hands, but fear gave him a strength he hadn't possessed before. "Please, Caper!"

Black dots floated in front of her eyes, and she wondered whether she was fainting.

Goff leaped down from the brick he was balanced on and pulled Caper's hands off T.C.'s arm. Caper catapulted backward, onto a slab of broken concrete, his mouth and eyes jarred wide open. Then Goff pushed aside the hunks of brickwork holding T.C.'s foot. The worst of the pain subsided, but her leg throbbed where she had scraped it on the bricks. She rolled up her trouser leg; already a bruise was blossoming on the shin, but she was surprised to see so little blood. She had expected a gusher.

Sprawled beside her on the bricks and concrete, Caper slashed the air with his fists and cried with angry, choking sobs.

"What's he making all that noise for?" asked Goff. "You're the one who got mashed."

"He's afraid." T.C. reached over to comfort Caper. She held his head against her chest, stroking his hair and brushing the tears from his sweaty dirt-streaked face.

"Weird, man," said Goff. "You're hurt, so you kiss him better!" T.C. held Caper until he was calm, brushed his hair back from his face, and kissed his sticky cheek. She felt as if Caper were her own brother.

Goff looked down on the pair of them. "Wouldn't've happened, if you hadn't been running away," he said. "What scared ya off? Nobody was gonna hurt ya."

She glared at him. "I *wasn't* scared."

"Looked like it to me."

"Well, I wasn't! I just decided I'd seen enough. I don't like wallowing in dirt."

Goff laughed: "Yeah? What do you think you're doing now?"

Without warning, a deep voice boomed out behind them:

"Who's that, Goff? Your girl friend?"

T.C. jumped and, in spite of her wounded leg, jerked around to confront the body connected to the voice. For a moment, she thought that Neil had tracked her down.

After the first shock, she realized that this old man didn't look like Neil at all. Only the first glimpse of the beard had made her think of Neil. This man was bald and his beard was gray and yellow; when he leered at her with his mouth in a lopsided grin, she could see that his teeth were brown and crooked. He wasn't anything like Neil.

"That's T.C.," said Goff. "And that's her brother. He's deaf and dumb."

"Hello, T.C.," said the old man. "Goff ain't very good with intros. I'm Moss. You know, like the stuff that grows on rocks and the sides of trees. I'm seventy-seven years old. How old're you?"

"Twelve."

"Got yourself a ways to go before you catch up with me. Hurt your leg?"

She shook her head.

"Just skinned my ankle." She stood up, but her ankle throbbed worse when she put her weight on it. "Nice to meet you. We've got to go now."

T.C. hadn't noticed that while she had been exploring the excavations and cave houses with Goff, the sky had been darkening. A raindrop splashed on her forehead and was followed immediately by three others and then by a cluster.

"Looks like we're gonna have us a storm," said the old man.

"Come on, Caper," said T.C., snatching his hand. "We've got to hurry."

"Where you going?"

The old man looked at her with shrewd gray eyes, as if he knew good and well that she didn't have a place to get out of the rain. She gestured toward Market Street, but he shook his head.

"Better stay here, with Goff and me. Until the rain passes."

T.C. didn't know what to do. She didn't want to crawl into one of those filthy underground hovels with these people she knew nothing about. But her ankle hurt and it was raining and she was miserable. Caper was whining and pushing at her with his fists. He didn't like standing in the rain.

"Sure, T.C. You can stay with me, like I said. Or with Moss. Moss lives next door. He ain't a slob like me. You oughta see how clean and nice his place is."

T.C. nodded and, clutching Caper's hand, limped over the bricks and concrete to the half-hidden cubicles tucked under the sidewalk.

7

If T.C. thought that she hadn't had much privacy in the commune, she discovered that she had no privacy at all living in the ruins of a demolished office building's basement with an old man and a teenage boy and God only knew how many other people wandering in and out of the shadows. She hadn't intended to move into one of the crumbling subterranean cubicles, but already two days had passed: two days and two nights in that dark, underground niche, among the rubbish left behind by previous squatters; two days and two nights of listening to the scuffling and gnawing of rodents and their battles with the ever-prowling cats.

"Some of these basements been here since the gold rush," Moss told her. "These here brick foundations, they're eighty, ninety, a hunnerd years old. Lookit them bricks; they don't make bricks like them no more."

T.C. listened to the old man, but she didn't care about antique bricks, not even about the gold rush. She watched him puffing on his battered pipe and rubbing his pockmarked face with his twisted fingers and wished that she could find a better place for Caper and her to live. She wasn't ungrateful to the old man, but she wished that he would leave her alone for a while.

She had run across several squatters living in these holes under the pavement and had glimpsed still others. Three days ago, she wouldn't have believed that human beings lived in places such as this, but here she was with Caper, in her own corner of a brick and concrete cave.

The favorite pastime of the squatters who lived in these secret caves was telling stories, and not stories about anything as long ago as the gold rush. These tales were about hard times and the unfairness of life and especially about the gangs that roamed the area, beating up people and robbing them. Everyone had a story to tell about a buddy or acquaintance who had got his skull air-conditioned with a piece of drainpipe or hunk of basalt.

So far, T.C. had been lucky, but she would have moved on if she had had a destination. That was the trouble: Once you settled in, it wasn't easy to pick up and go look for another place to crash. Caper seemed to like living in the ruins, looking for the cats and watching the pigeons. It was a game for him.

A game. This was no game for her. She was scared, and the worst part of it was that she couldn't admit it. She had to tough it out, the way she toughed out everything in her life, with her wisecracks and smart-aleck attitude that made people so mad at her. This shield that she was trying desperately to keep in place was her own protection. At times, she suspected that Goff saw around the crumbling edges of her shield, but she pretended that it was invulnerable and pushed her real feelings even deeper into herself.

She couldn't keep the people back home from crowding into her thoughts. What would they have said if they could have seen where she was camping? She would have enjoyed watching her mother's face, or Malvina's, as the women confronted the heap of rags and rubble where she and Caper slept.

T.C. sat on a stack of concrete fragments in the sun, scratching herself (it had been days since she had had a bath). Already, she was becoming accustomed to this life. Even to the dirt.

"I guess you can become used to anything," she said to a couple of pigeons tugging at a filthy scrap of rag.

Every morning, she went up to the grocery store on Mission and bought food for herself and Caper. She had to buy it every day because there was no place to store it. Not where it wouldn't spoil or be found by the cats and rats and other squatters. She slept with her money in her underwear, and never told anybody how much she had. Whenever Caper and T.C. ate, that boy, Goff, managed to come by, and she always gave him something. It didn't hurt to have friends.

As it was, she didn't sleep deeply when she did doze off, and she was more protective of Caper than ever, more like a mother than a sister. She could only rest if he was next to her, and even so she fell in and out of dreams all night, as she might have fallen in and out of spiraling memories or visions of the future. The fearful morning would swirl around her and she would stalk around the cave, shaking a cramp out of one grubby foot or trying to comb the snarls out of her filthy hair. Sometimes, in a fit of anger at what she had done to herself and to Caper, she would kick at the abandoned cigarette packs and beer cans on the uneven floor and declare that she would do something to escape this place. But where? Her imagination failed her when she tried to think of an alternative.

One solution was offered her the second or third morning she went out to buy food. She had to pass half a dozen young people in robes and turbans and bare feet lounging in a doorway near the store. When she came out of the grocery, one of the young men jumped in front of her. He looked like a character out of an old adventure movie, one of those pictures filled with geniis and flying carpets and thieves on camelback.

"Praise God!" he shouted.

"Praise God!" echoed the others, except for the baby nursing in public at its teenage mother's breast.

"We seen you before, sister," said the young man. He was kind of cute, but his expression seemed flat, as if something had happened to wash away most of his personality. "We decided we got to help you."

"Come with us and God will provide!" urged a girl only a few years older than T.C., draped in soiled white sheets and a lopsided turban from underneath which a strand of red hair trailed. Her eyes also looked washed out, and her voice, although fervent, seemed flat and dead.

"We got a house," explained the young man who had surprised her. "And a vegetable garden and we're going to have goats too."

"And a pig," called out the girl with the baby. "Don't forget the pig."

"We are a port in a storm, a corral for strays, a haven from the corrupt and unholy world!"

T.C. had never been religious, but she would have been willing to go with these toga-draped young fanatics if she had thought they could help her to provide a better life for Caper. Standing in the middle of the sidewalk, she clutched her small bag of groceries and listened to their declarations and urgings, but couldn't bring herself to trust them. She had left one commune; she didn't need to hook up with another. And they might doublecross her, call her parents or the cops, or even attract the cops to Caper and her. No, she preferred to go it alone.

"Praise God!" came the chorus from the sheet-wrapped figures sprawled in the doorway. Most of them, as far as she could tell, didn't have anything on under those sheets. In a couple of cases, it was more than obvious.

"No," she murmured, backing away from the vacant-eyed, costumed group. "No, thanks, I don't want to."

"Come on, kid. God wants you to join up with us."

She shook her head, stepping off the curb into the street get away from the young man blocking her path. A girl had maneuvered behind her, but T.C. dodged her, too, and broke into a run. She darted around the corner, pursued by a final cry of "Praise the Lord God!"

After that morning, T.C. avoided that block and grocery store; she found another market in which to buy her scanty supplies.

Most of the people who lived in the San Francisco catacombs were men. T.C. spied only a couple of women among the ruins, and they were old and raggedy. With her short hair and jeans and bulky jacket, T.C. looked like a boy, especially with the recently acquired layer of dirt.

"You better let everybody think you and him is brothers," Goff told her. "Know what I mean? It's safer that way."

One of the women picked her way across the open lot. Hunched over like a witch, rags trailing around her like leaves, she looked more like a windblown shrub than a human being. Her gray hair stuck out in tendrils beneath her old felt hat and a collection of ragged skirts blossomed like bunches of leaves over an ancient pair of men's trousers. Since her clothes were castoffs that she found in her wanderings, it wasn't surprising that they disintegrated almost as fast as she picked them up. Every time T.C. glimpsed the woman, she had either added or shed fragments of herself. Yesterday, she had been plodding over the rubble in a pair of decaying rubber boots, but today she hiked along in faded yellow men's sneakers. Sweaters and shawls hung in tatters from her back. She carried a red Emporium shopping bag that bulged with the treasures of her day's scavanging.

"Stay clear of Bernie," Goff cautioned her. "She's a holy terror. Hates everybody, but especially girls."

T.C. made no move to greet the mumbling hag, but when she was directly opposite T.C., the woman stopped, stared at her, and spit on the ground before continuing on her zigzag course toward a crumbling doorway in a far corner of the ruins.

How did people like Bernie and Moss end up squatting in these brick and concrete ruins? What went wrong with their lives? It was scary to think about: Could anybody lose everything and fall to a place like this? Or did these people live here because they liked it? It was hard to believe that a human being would choose this life. Maybe some of them were runaways, too. Could adults be runaways? What were they running away from? Not from parents. From husbands and wives? From jobs? From the police?

T.C. had never wrestled with ideas like these before. She didn't know how to handle them. Although it was easier to give up and live from day to day, she wanted to figure things out for herself. She and Caper couldn't stay here indefinitely. This was only a temporary solution. She couldn't forget that Caper depended on her.

"There's nothing to be afraid of," she told herself. "Caper and me, we're doing fine."

She didn't hear the footsteps coming up behind her. "Talkin' to yourself?"

Goff hunkered down on a rock beside her. He didn't smell any better than he had when she had first encountered him, but she guessed she was getting used to him, because she didn't feel so much like holding her nose when he was around. Or maybe she was starting to smell, too, and didn't notice his stink.

"I was wondering about old Bernie. How she came to be living down here."

Goff shrugged his shoulders. "Who cares? She's just an old boozer."

"She drinks?"

"Anything she can get hold of. Cleaning fluid. Turpentine. You name it. Her place is wall-to-wall bottles. If she can't buy it, she steals it."

T.C. had never stolen anything in her life except the food and clothes for Caper. And the money from Neil's box. The money had changed her life. She couldn't go back even if she wanted to. Stealing that fifty dollars had cut her off from honest people. They wouldn't want her in the commune. She didn't belong to anyone, except Caper.

"Cold?" T.C. looked up at Goff and nodded, hugging herself. "I know something that'll make you shake even more. A blind guy got beat up last night. Some thugs who been cruisin' around here got him over on Mission. Broke his arm and cracked his skull. Almost wasted him."

"Why?"

"Why? Why you think? Plain meanness."

"But they couldn't have got much money, not from a blind man."

"Few dollars. Enough to buy a beer, maybe. I told ya, T.C., they like beating up folks. Robbing 'em is like, you know, an excuse."

A shudder ran the length of T.C.'s body.

"Hey, I told ya I knew something that'd make you shake, and it did!" Goff grinned, showing his broken yellow teeth. "You better be careful, T.C. Anybody finds out you got money, you're gonna be in trouble."

"I don't have any money!"

"Yeah. I know. But, listen, there're plenty o' mean bastards who'd as soon knock your teeth in as look at you. You got money, so much the better for 'em. You don't, they'll still bash your head in. Watch where you hang out, okay? Even if they think you're a dude, you're still pretty small."

"You're not so big!"

"No, but I'm mean! I know how to fight dirty."

T.C. nodded. "I'll bet you do, too."

T.C. sat on a rock in the sun near the place she shared with Caper and the old man, staring at a rusty tennis ball can half-buried under a pile of broken bricks. She was feeling blue, because she had spent at least an hour trying to communicate—really communicate—with Caper, and all that had happened was that he had got impatient and pushed her away and stomped back into the room behind the cardboard partition.

It wasn't supposed to work out like this. Caper was supposed to get well and they were supposed to be happy together. Already, she was beginning to wish that they hadn't run away, and that made her feel guilty, because she had had no choice but to rescue Caper from his stepfather, and it wasn't his fault that everything had got screwed up.

She gave the tennis ball can a kick and went off to look for

Goff. She found him in his hovel, warming a stinking fluid over a smoking fire.

"Will you look after Caper for a while?" she asked, watching him pour the foul, dark liquid from the hot tin into another, equally filthy, can. "I have to buy some food and a newspaper. I'm going to look through the want ads."

Goff's grimy features twisted into an expression of disbelief. "Why?"

"To find a job. How can we live if I don't get work?"

"Don't be stupid, T.C. Who's gonna hire a twelve-year-old? Besides, kids can't get jobs without a work permit."

"I'll do what you said. I'll say I'm eighteen."

"Yeah? That don't work when it comes to jobs. Somebody hires you, see, first thing you know he's got the law on his butt."

He sniffed happily at his concoction, sipped at it, then took a big swallow.

"Want some?"

He held out the can to her. She shook her head.

"Okay." Indifferent to her refusal, he gulped down the rest of the steaming liquid.

"Goff, what was that stuff?"

"This is my own invention. You take all the leftovers you can find and heat 'em up together. You can swallow anything, if it's hot enough. This here was old coffee, port wine, chicken noodle soup, and stewed tomatoes. Warmed the old gut!"

Even after her recent experiences in the city, T.C. couldn't understand Goff. She had never gone hungry in the way that he had. She had skipped meals, accidentally or intentionally, but she had never wondered where her next meal was coming from. Even now, with her resources limited and sure to run out, the prospect of hunger was only an idea to her, not a reality. It wouldn't be a reality until she had lived with it.

"My newspaper," she said. "I've got to get my newspaper."

"Okay. I'll watch the kid. He likes me. We don't talk much, but he grins a lot. And I show him how to do things, like building forts with bricks. And how to play follow the leader. You know something? He never played it before. But he ain't as dumb as he looks."

"Thanks. I appreciate it. I'll buy you something."

"Buy a beer for Moss, too. He'd like that. If you got the bread."

"Maybe."

She hiked across the rubble-strewn lot until she came to a roughly marked trail that led up to a hole in the fence. Passing the excavation in which old Bernie lived, she glanced over just as the old woman peeked out from behind her ragged curtain. When Bernie realized that she had been spotted, she spat on the ground and jumped back into the shadows.

In the grocery store several blocks away on Folsom, T.C. bought an *Examiner*, a package of Oreos, bologna, crackers, low-fat milk, and two Hamm's beers. The clerk hesitated before ringing up the beers, but T.C. explained, "They're for my dad. He's sick and can't come himself." He looked around the empty store, shrugged his shoulders, and added the cost of the beers to the total.

T.C. hiked back to the site of the excavations, shifting the bag from one arm to the other as her muscles tired. She ducked down through the hole in the storm fence and hurried through the rubble, scaring several pigeons and the skinniest, saddest excuse for a kitten she had ever seen. She was crunching through the gravel and broken bricks past old Bernie's place when the old woman burst out from behind her tattered curtains, screaming and waving her arms. She looked like a scarecrow that had come to life through the power of black magic.

"What the hell you think you're doin', spyin' on me? Get the hell outta here! I won't have no little snots spyin' on me. Who you think you are?"

Her rags flapping and dancing around her dumpy little body, the old woman jumped up and down, waving her red-knuckled fists at T.C. The girl stared with amazement at the spectacle.

"Get away from here! You can't spy on me!"

"But I wasn't!" protested T.C. "I don't know what you—"

The old woman bent down and plucked a brick shard from the rubble at her feet and hurled it at T.C. The throw went wild, but T.C. moved away, just in case the next shot might be more accurate.

"I wasn't spying!" she shouted, but old Bernie picked up another hunk of brick with both hands and hurled it in the same general direction. It shot past T.C.'s head with only inches to spare.

"Okay, if that's the way you want it to be!"

The girl ran around the edge of the excavations, toward the row of caves that she shared with Moss and Goff. The old woman heaved one last piece of brick with such fury that she lost her balance and fell over backward in a tangle of skirts and rags and an explosion of obscenities. T.C. fled to her own hideaway, clutching the grocery bag with sweaty hands.

"Here's your beer," she told Goff, thrusting a can at Goff. "And one for Moss. The guy in the store looked at me pretty funny when I bought 'em."

"He let you do it, didn't he? You can't go around being afraid, T.C. You gotta bluff your way through, make the other sap back down. That's the way to get by in the world."

Goff called to Moss and gave him the beer. The old man elaborately thanked T.C. and, with much ceremony, popped the top off the can. T.C. told them about Bernie.

"Always said she was nuts," pronounced Goff.

"It's old age," said Moss. "Some women get that way. One dame I knew took after her husband with a meat cleaver. Chased him all around the kitchen and cut off his left thumb. Bernie, there, she never was too damn bright. Probably what few brains she had are turnin' to mush."

"You ask me," volunteered Goff, "she's just pickled."

T.C. hated the nights in the cave. The darkness, the desolation, the lack of security even in the back of the cave on her roughly made bed, made her reluctant to risk sleep.

Goff tried to talk her out of her fears. "You don't got to be afraid of the dark, T.C. You gotta understand, it's your friend. It's like a blanket, all rich and thick and I know I'm safe, all wrapped up in it. Look at it this way, T.C.: If you can't see nobody, then nobody can see you, neither. Ain't that right? It just depends on stayin' cool and lettin' your eyes adjust and being perfectly quiet until you make your move—*if* you want to make a move. Sometimes you do, sometimes you don't. Me, I know my way around this place in the blackest black. I ain't a bit afraid down here. This is my territory. I'm like one of them cats. Even when I'm asleep, I'm ready to jump up and leap into action. Anybody else who comes down here, he don't know his way around, see, because it ain't his territory. That's how we got the advantage, even in the pitch black."

T.C. wished it were that easy.

That night, Goff and Moss and T.C. concocted a feast by pooling their supplies. T.C. contributed Oreo cookies, crackers, and bologna, Goff contributed a can of beef stew he had shoplifted, and Moss gave half a box of chocolate-covered cherries and half a pint of sweet port wine. Only Goff and Moss drank the wine, but Caper cried when the chocolate-covered cherries were gone. It took a fistful of Oreos to make him stop. He pulled apart the cookies, scraped off all of the white frosting, rolled it together into a ball of gray with the dirt from his hands and popped it into his mouth before eating any of the chocolate halves.

Moss cut up the bologna and added it to the stew when he heated it over the camp fire. He even poured a dollop of wine into the pot. He said it would help them to sleep. T.C. was surprised: The finished product didn't taste half bad.

Lights and fires after dark were risky, T.C. had learned, because they might attract the law. As dusk deepened the shadows the inhabitants of the caves retreated to their beds. T.C. and Caper crawled into their sleeping bag in a dark corner and huddled together.

That night T.C. realized that she resented being stuck with Caper. She did care about him and did want to find a way for him to have a life where he wouldn't have to fear getting beat up, but she wished that she hadn't had to be the one to rescue him.

She tried to make herself feel sentimental about Caper, telling herself how cute he was, and how sweet, but he wasn't that cute, really, and he definitely wasn't sweet. He was a dirty little kid with a lot of problems, and she was stuck with him.

She slept eventually, but several times she woke up, listened groggily to the rumble of night traffic, and then drifted off again. In her half-wakeful state, her arm around

Caper's skinny body, the warmth of their flesh confined in the sleeping bag, she felt surprisingly secure. She gave him comfort, but his presence helped to dissolve her fears, too.

She had dozed off again, after watching the shadows on the brick wall and listening to horns and sirens in the distance, when a scream cut through the night. Her head jerked up and her eyes opened as the scream assaulted the darkness again. A cry for help clawing at the night: the shrill and ragged scream of someone being attacked.

Deep in the sleeping bag, T.C. and Caper clung to each other. They heard the sound of scuffling and of somebody running over the bricks and broken concrete; pieces of rubble were knocked over, and somebody cursed. Another brief cry of pain: a needle in the night. Then the scream stopped. Only after she no longer heard it did T.C. realize that it had been a woman calling for help.

It must have been old Bernie. Someone must have gone after poor old Bernie.

Only the warmth, the nearness, of Caper's body kept T.C. from slipping over the edge into ice-cold panic. Was somebody going from cubicle to cubicle, attacking all of the people camping in the excavations? Those thugs Goff had warned her about? What if she and Caper were next? What would she do? What could she do?

She wanted to find out what had happened, to know if it was over, but she didn't want to draw attention to herself. Maybe whoever it was, the thug or gang, didn't know she and Caper were there. So she lay frozen for what were the longest minutes of her life, her ears straining to recognize and interpret each sound.

Caper whimpered, but she put her hand over his mouth and hugged him tightly.

Crunch . . . crunch . . . crunch . . . Somebody was walking toward them: a brick tumbled down from a piece of broken wall . . . more footsteps . . . crunch . . . crunch . . . stopping just the other side of the half-wall behind which she lay with Caper. Her body rigid, pressed against Caper, her jaw trembling as she tried to control her terror, she waited.

Then two more steps and a figure silhouetted against the night: "T.C.? You there?"

Goff. She could breathe again. "Yes." Her voice sounded tiny, even to herself.

Goff crouched beside the sleeping bag. "You okay?"

"Yeah. Sure."

"Some guys, they was running in and out of the places along here, ripping off folks, beating 'em up. They got old Bernie."

"I heard."

"They didn't come in here?"

"N . . . n . . . no."

"You were lucky. They whacked Moss a good one. But I think they killed Bernie. Blood all over the place. They must've used a pipe or a hunk of concrete. Jesus, I never saw nobody look like that before. Moss went to call an ambulance. She ain't gonna make it. They busted her head wide open."

The rest of the night was crowded with sounds of police cars and ambulances, floodlights swinging like shards of daylight in and out of the cubicles. Some of the cave-dwellers picked up their belongings and fled, others burrowed deeper into their holes. Even before the streaked gray of dawn began to pick out the shapes of the skyscrapers in the financial district, the newspaper and TV crews invaded the scene. The murder and the description of the subterranean village would give folks something to read over breakfast, something to listen to while preparing for work.

"You and him better get out," Goff told T.C. "Before you get picked up by you know who."

"We haven't done anything."

"You're underage, ain't ya? They'll take you to juvie. You want to get locked up with a bunch of freaks? Get out of here. Come back later, when the cops and reporters have split."

T.C. hustled Caper out of the sleeping bag, rolled it up, packed their few belongings, and led the groggy boy into the chilly morning. They crawled across the lot, keeping low behind the largest piles of rubble, maneuvered up to the street, then inched through one of the holes in the storm fence. They didn't stop walking until they came to a park across the street from the adobe mission that had been the beginning of the city two hundred years before. They sat under a palm tree and watched the sun struggle into the sky.

T.C. held Caper's bony hand in her fist and stared at the dog shit and cigar butts and soggy candy wrappers on the ground in front of the bench. An old man shuffling past coughed loudly and spat a huge greenish glob on the pavement. T.C. couldn't stop shivering. She knew it was because of old Bernie: The woman hadn't been anything to her, but the picture of Bernie's head smashed into mush paralyzed her.

Old Bernie. Just a drunk, nobody who mattered, but T.C. felt sick. She wouldn't have minded Bernie yelling and cursing and throwing hunks of brick at her again, if the old bat could have been brought back to life. It wasn't Bernie's fault if she was an ill-tempered old lush. She couldn't have been happy living like that.

"I wonder when it'll be safe to go back?" T.C. wondered. "Maybe we shouldn't go back at all."

She looked at Caper, as if she expected him to reply, but he wiped his nose on his sleeve and huddled against her shoulder. He was tired and afraid. Maybe all of the commotion had reminded him of his mother and stepfather. Maybe he was afraid that she was going to take him back to them. But she could only guess what was going through his head.

"Don't worry, Caper," she whispered, stroking his shaggy head. "I'll take care of you."

Should they return to the excavations? Those ruins were the only home they had in San Francisco, the friends they had there the only friends they had, yet she was afraid to go back. There had to be a better place, if only she could find it.

She thought of Goff and wondered what he would do. He seemed to like living in those brick and concrete caves, and to enjoy prowling around among the ruins of the flattened buildings.

But there was nothing to take T.C. and Caper back there, nothing except their relationship with Goff and Moss. And, after all, she didn't know if she could really trust them. They had educated her about living the life of a squatter in the rubble, had wised her up about the dangers, but she had paid them back, all right, with food and beer and things. It wasn't as if they had done it out of the bigness of their hearts. She wasn't dumb enough to think they cared about her or Caper.

Yet they were the only people in San Francisco she could turn to for help.

Another old man shuffled past, plucking the chewed stub of a cigar from his purple lips and dropping it at the foot of the palm tree beside the bench. T.C. averted her gaze to the earth-colored mission and the pink oleanders growing around it. What was going to become of Caper and her? Whatever she did, she'd screw up somehow, but she couldn't screw up worse than old Bernie. Adults liked to say how important experience was, didn't they? Okay, she was getting plenty of experience, so she was bound to end up educated as all hell.

But where did that leave her?

Sitting on a park bench opposite a two-hundred-year-old church with a skinny kid who happened to have cigarette burns all over his body and a scab three inches across the top of his head.

That's where it left her.

8

A fat brown-skinned woman in a brightly patterned red and black skirt flaring wide over her hips and a low-cut blouse that revealed puckered, olive-hued cleavage herded several small children past the bench on which T.C. and Caper sat, shouting Spanish and gesturing angrily with her short-fingered, pudgy hands. The children trotted on their short legs, playing hide and seek around the woman's skirt and behind the bench and palm tree.

T.C. watched the woman steer the children across the street and around the corner, like John Wayne herding two thousand longhorn steers on a massive Technicolor cattle drive, and wanted to cry.

For all her scolding and shouting, that woman was happy. She had a place. She was a woman with kids: they were her responsibility. She wasn't rich or glamorous or famous, but T.C. envied her. At that moment, T.C. would have envied just about anybody who walked past.

That woman lived in a house, had a husband, friends, belonged. Somehow, T.C. had slipped loose from society. She didn't belong. She felt as if she were sliding down the mirrorlike side of a glacier and dead ahead was a jagged crack that dropped straight down to the center of the earth. This desperate feeling made T.C. afraid she was going to do something dumb, like jump up and rush over to some stranger and cling to him or beg him to take her home.

She couldn't go it alone. She wasn't strong enough. She needed a friend, somebody to talk to and turn to when she was in trouble.

She pulled on the backpack, stood up, took Caper's hand and began walking. When they neared the blocks of excavations, T.C. detoured up and down the side streets, peering around grubby old buildings, trying to figure out if any cops or TV mobile units were still prowling around. When she had satisfied herself that everything down in the hole was back to normal, she led Caper into the ruins. He seemed glad to be climbing over the rubble again.

Like a straggly-bearded Buddha, Moss squatted beneath a jagged concrete overhang, a foul-smelling mixture sending up black clouds from his old pipe. T.C. had to admit to herself that she was happy to see him again.

"It's okay, kid," the old man told her. "They poked their noses all over the damn place, but they've cleared out." He motioned for her to come closer. "Bernie croaked. Them guys that did it got a murder rap hanging over their heads now."

"Police catch them yet?"

Moss shook his head. The veins in his nose pulsated with righteous anger.

"Nah. They're in L.A. by now. But I can tell you one thing. Wherever they are, they ain't gonna be comin' round here no more."

"T.C.!" Goff bounced like a mountain goat over the

canyons of rubble and threw his arms around her. He didn't smell any better than before.

"Thought you wasn't comin' back!"

T.C. shrugged her shoulders: "Didn't have anyplace else to go. Not anyplace special, I mean."

Caper almost exploded with joy at seeing Goff again. Making little chirping noises, he tugged on the fourteen-year-old's outer layer of clothing. Goff ruffled the kid's hair and wrestled with him. T.C. saw how careful Goff was not to hurt Caper as they rolled in the dirt. He cared about Caper, T.C. realized, and fought off a twinge of jealousy.

That evening, Goff invited T.C. to take her things over to his cave and sleep there.

"You and him both. I can make room for you real easy, so you won't have to be alone."

"You only gotta move a few feet if you can bear to be around an old man," said Moss. "I'm gonna be seventy-eight in January, but if somebody tries to get smart with us, I'll show 'em a thing or two." He poked his pipe in the air. "I was a boxer—fought for money. Won a few bouts, too. I worked on railroads and oil rigs in my day. That takes a real man. I'm strong for my age, but I used to have iron muscles."

He shoved out his gut and scowled at the rubble around him.

"You still look like a tough old fart," said Goff, tapping Moss with his fist in the vicinity beneath the old man's streaked beard.

"Ha!" snorted Moss. "I eat squirts like you for breakfast!"

T.C. felt a burst of affection for the old man. He was an odd old guy, not like Neil at all, yet her feelings toward Neil had transferred to him. If he was gruff and vulgar and dirty, well, he had had a hard life. Seventy-seven was a pretty old age to reach when you had been poor all your life. He was entitled to be grumpy and to brag a little.

She looked from Moss to Goff and back again, and unwrapped herself from around the fear that had been so heavy within her. "Okay, Moss," she said. "I guess Caper and me'd feel better if we moved in with you."

The old man nodded and jerked a thumb toward the cubicle that he had long ago claimed as his.

"Bring your stuff on in. Pick yourself an empty spot."

T.C. felt like hugging that old man, felt like shouting to the whole city from the top of Coit Tower what a kind, generous old man he was.

A Coca-Cola advertisement, ancient on rusted tin, greeted T.C. when she carried her backpack and sleeping bag into Moss's cave, deep beneath the concrete overhang that remained from the ground floor of a building razed half a decade ago. He had found the six-foot-long sign in an empty lot and had dragged it here to keep the wind and rain off his bed. The seat from an old car was propped against one rough brick wall, with a square of paint-splattered canvas in front of it for a rug. Beyond, against the farthest wall, she saw a sleeping arrangement made up of an old mattress and random coverings acquired over the years. None of them would have qualified as a real blanket, but they managed to keep him from freezing at night.

"Never tried to get myself anything worth more'n two cents," Moss told T.C. " 'Cause then, sure enough, somebody'll bust in and steal it. The best way to be happy is to never have nothing anybody else'll want to take away from you."

Involuntarily, T.C.'s hand touched through her T-shirt the money that she had left: almost forty dollars in cash. She knew it was a lot to be carrying around and never mentioned it to anybody, but she wouldn't have been surprised if some of the other squatters didn't suspect she had it, maybe more than she really did have. Of course, she wasn't worried about Goff and Moss. They were buddies.

Her eyes traveled from Moss's streaked beard, down his shapeless coat, past a button hanging by a single thread to his greasy and mud-caked trousers with the torn cuffs and his battered, cracked shoes. One of the shoes was laced with a piece of blackened string, the other had no lace at all. Her gaze returned to his gray, veined face, and she thought with sudden sadness that he was *old*. The word filled with meaning for her perhaps for the first time. Old meant almost dead. That was the significance of the wrinkles and the gray and white hair and the stooped back and twisted limbs: death. It shocked and frightened her. Moss had been a baby back about the time when Teddy Roosevelt was President. It was scary to think about. She could see herself old and wrinkled and getting ready to die, to stop existing.

T.C. made an elaborate show of arranging the sleeping bag and backpack on the ground beside a small piece of brick wall. This new home wasn't very spacious, but most of the time she and Caper would be outside, doing things. That was what life was: doing things, finding out about the world.

Moss stood in front of her scratching his almost bald, freckled head. "I was thinking, T.C., if you got any money, or anything valuable, maybe you oughta hide it. You shouldn't keep it in your backpack. That's right where somebody'd look, if somebody—I ain't sayin' who, but somebody—was fixin' to rob you."

T.C. nodded. "I don't have it in the backpack. I sort of carry it with me. I mean, it isn't very much, but it's in my underwear. I figure that's as safe as anyplace."

Moss raised his shaggy gray-white eyebrows.

"Mebbe . . . and mebbe not."

"But . . ." The girl looked around her, at the brick walls and collapsed hunks of foundation. "Where? Where could I hide it?"

"There's places. You'd be surprised, girlie. There're nooks and crannies nobody'd think of. *I* know."

"Well . . ." said T.C. doubtfully. "If you think so . . ."

The old man and the young girl confronted each other, each trying to determine what was going on in the other's head.

"Never mind," barked Moss, "if you don't trust me."

He turned away with an angry shrug, looking down at a yellowed crumpled newspaper on the dirt floor.

"It's not that!" said T.C. "It's just, well, I'm nervous. If anything happened to the money, I don't know what Caper and I would do. I'm not old enough to work, and he depends on me. I'm afraid somebody'll find the money if we hide it."

"I guarantee, little lady, I can put it in a spot where nobody'll ever find it."

T.C. looked into Moss's craggy face. She couldn't let him think that she didn't trust him. "Okay," she said, at last.

She unbuttoned her jacket and reached in, groping beneath her T-shirt. A moment later her hand emerged, a small wad of paper money in it.

"It's only about thirty dollars."

"Only! I ain't seen thirty bucks at one time in years. Not for years!"

His hand, calloused and freckled and covered with white hairs, reached out. It was trembling, from some kind of palsy or old age or maybe just from excitement.

T.C. dropped the money into his palm.

"Come," he said. "I'll show you the safest place in San Francisco to put it. Safer than the Bank of America! Safer than the vault at the U.S. Mint!"

Like two conspirators, they glanced over their shoulders and shuffled into the dark corner at the rear of the cubicle.

"I dug this secret place out myself, when I first moved into here. Not another human being knows about it. You're the first person I ever showed it to."

T.C. tried to appear appropriately appreciative, but the old man wasn't looking at her.

Mumbling to himself, he lifted some bricks from the ancient foundation wall, reached into a narrow, dark hole, and pulled out a little tin box. The box was old and dirty, but looked as if it might once have held English tea. Although smaller, it reminded T.C. of the other box, in Neil's desk. He pulled off the lid and looked inside the box. It was empty.

"Been a long time since I had anything worth hiding."

He dropped the folded ten-dollar bills into the box, secured the lid, and pushed it back into the narrow opening in the wall. With T.C. watching, he replaced the bricks, tapping them with his broad fist to wedge them into place.

"There! Would anybody know there was a treasure in that wall?"

T.C. shook her head. It seemed a safe enough place.

As they walked outside, the old man rested a heavy paw on her shoulder. "Don't worry, girlie, old Moss is gonna take care of ya."

She looked up at his parchment-skinned face, with the coarse white and gray hair sticking out in all directions in odd little tufts, and smiled. He was ugly, but goodhearted, and that was what mattered.

She reached up and pulled his face down to hers. It was a

form of self-discipline that she was imposing on herself. She had to do it, to prove that she didn't dislike him and distrust him because he was old and ugly. She kissed his leathery cheek.

Up close, he didn't smell much better than Goff.

"Thanks," she said, squeezing his rough-skinned hand with her small, soft hand.

"I'm an old bastard," he protested, "but I got a soft spot for pretty young girls!"

He gave her a Groucho Marx leer and slowly lowered his bulk onto a mound of concrete slabs in front of his cubicle.

Suddenly, T.C. felt a need to see her father and Neil again. And her mom, too. Even old Malvina. She wished that she had thought to bring photographs of them. Just a snapshot or two. But she had been in too much of a hurry to think about that.

She remembered how she had always answered her parents or Neil and Malvina, even when they tried to be understanding, with a wisecrack. Always trying to show off how smart she was; it had become such a habit that she hadn't even known she was doing it. They must have hated her. She wanted to tell them that she was sorry. She hadn't meant to be such a pain in the neck. She didn't know why she had run around shooting off her mouth and losing her temper, but if she ever went back she would try to act more human. Of course, she wasn't going back, so it was a waste of time to think about it.

If she went home, Caper would be sent to his mother and stepfather, and she couldn't let that happen.

She glanced at Moss, hunched over on his concrete slab. The flesh dropped from the bones of his face like hunks of gray clay. He realized that she was looking at him and, without raising his eyes, murmured:

"I can't get ole Bernie outta my brain." He pulled a filthy bandana handkerchief out of his hip pocket and rubbed his nose and forehead with it. "Can't get used to the idea that the ole tramp is lyin' in the morgue."

"What's going to happen to her?"

"A pauper's grave. At city expense. Nobody ain't gonna come out and claim her withered ole body, you can bet your bottom dollar on that. Who'd want to admit he was related to that rumpot?"

T.C. nodded. Was he thinking about himself, too, when he said that? Was he figuring that he would be buried at city expense in a pauper's grave? It wasn't much of an end to look forward to.

That night, Moss collected contributions and, while everyone sat around the open campfire in front of his cubicle, cooked a fragrant Mulligan stew. Besides Moss, there were Goff, T.C. and Caper, a couple of young guys who had wandered into town and found their way to the excavations, much as Caper and T.C. had, and another old guy by the name of Krementz. He was from someplace in Europe, this old man, and didn't speak good English, but his courtly manners and a sad, defeated expression, T.C. thought, made him look like a man who had once been rich and then had lost everything. He wouldn't talk about himself, so T.C. never found out if her suspicion was true.

They didn't talk much, but when they did it was about Bernie and her fate. Each person there, except maybe Caper, wondered if he or she would come to a sudden, violent end. Life, it seemed, was like that: Someone could bop you on the head or rip out your guts, and that was that.

The fire died down, the stew was eaten, but no one made a move to leave. Each person seemed to be trying to avoid the moment when he or she must be alone. Finally, that moment could be held off no longer, and Goff and then old Krementz and the others wandered into the dark. Moss wished T.C. and Caper good night and crawled among his rags. T.C. and Caper wriggled into their sleeping bag and, to the sounds of the city above them, gradually forgot their fears enough to sleep.

The next day, T.C. caught herself scratching so hard through her clothes that she drew blood. Right then, she decided that it was time to find a laundromat. Hiding behind a half wall of bricks, she stripped off her clothes and put on the somewhat less filthy ones that she had been carrying around. Then she went after Caper. He didn't want to change his clothes—maybe he had grown to like dirt—but she persisted and, eventually, got him out of the foul things he had been wearing and into the one other outfit she had brought for him. She wadded everything up and wrapped it with her shirt into a compact bundle.

Neither Moss nor Goff could tell T.C. where to find a laundromat. They didn't understand why she wanted one. Seemed like a waste of money to them. So, taking Caper by the hand and slinging the bundle over her shoulder, she set off on her own to search for a coin-op laundry.

They hadn't gone more than a couple of blocks when a whirring sound coming up behind them on the sidewalk made Caper jerk his hand away from T.C. and jump around as if he expected a bus to be driving right down the pavement toward him.

"Caper! What's the matter with you?"

Then she saw what had set him off and her own stomach did a flip-flop. A man in a motorized wheelchair was chugging along behind them. A second glance told T.C. that the man wasn't Caper's stepfather, but, uttering that hoarse, animal sound that he made when he was terrified, Caper struggled to break free and run away.

"It's okay, Caper!" She pulled him into a doorway. "It's not who you think it is!"

The wheelchair putt-putted up the block, the long-haired young man slouched in it scowling at T.C. and Caper. When he reached them, he raised his one good arm (the other one, withered, lay like a dead animal on his lap) in an angry gesture.

"Why don't you teach him that cripples ain't freaks, huh? You think 'cause I'm a cripple I'm some kind of monster? You make me sick."

"No! You don't understand. He thought you were somebody else. It wasn't anything personal."

"Go to hell!"

The young man pushed a button on his control panel and the wheelchair turned and scooted down the concrete ramp at the corner and into the street. Still muttering to himself, the man chugged against the light, into the middle of the traffic lanes. Car squealed to a halt and drivers cursed while the wheelchair inched across the street and up the ramp on the opposite side.

Only when the traffic separated them from the man in the wheelchair would Caper stop crying. Then he grabbed T.C. by the sleeve and pulled her in the opposite direction from that taken by the motorized wheelchair.

The second door around the corner turned out to be what they were looking for: "Put Your Duds in Our Suds!"

A small neighborhood laundromat, completely self-service, with an orange cardboard jack-o'-lantern and a life-sized cardboard skeleton taped to the dirty plate-glass window.

Halloween!

T.C. had forgotten that it would soon be Halloween, but confronting the faded jack-o'-lantern and lopsided skeleton, she was assaulted by memories of past Halloweens and the plans she had made for this one.

The kids decorated the commune for holidays. They had a good time doing it, especially on Halloween. They always had a big Halloween party, with a haunted house. The older kids took over the library and transformed it with snakes hanging from the ceiling, skeletons that glowed in the dark, monsters that rose out of the black, and a terrifying maze alive with spooky surprises, and then guided the younger kids through the delicious horrors. It made T.C. laugh, how much the little ones loved to be scared. But she would miss all of that, this year.

Untying the bundle she had made with her shirt, T.C. pushed the filthy clothes into one of the smaller washing machines, bought a quarter package of soap and poured it in, and slammed the door. She put the money in the coin slot and showed Caper how to slide it in. He made a tentative, halfhearted attempt, and she pantomimed that he should do it more forcefully, so he gave it a fierce shove and the machine jerked into action. Water poured in with a great rush and suds began rising. Caper edged forward, peering at the eyeball-like window on the front of the machine. He watched the churning suds and the clothes tumbling around and around, and grinned at T.C., proud that he had been the one to cause all of this to happen.

A middle-aged woman sitting in a plastic and chromium chair in front of the window, while her clothes spun in one of the dryers, was the only other customer in the laundromat. She was crocheting a fancy square covered with tight little flowers and curlicue leaves; T.C. didn't see how the woman could manage such ornate and detailed work without going blind. The jack-o'-lantern on the window seemed to be staring with disbelief over the woman's shoulder at her flashing hands. Beside her, on the window ledge, a plastic-cased portable radio was tuned to a station that played old-time songs like *Night and Day* and *It Had to Be you* and *Secret Love*. She looked up from her crocheted flowers and leaves and smiled when T.C. and Caper put their clothes in a machine. She seemed to think it was cute, the two of them doing their laundry together.

T.C. and Caper sat on a couple of chairs across the room, facing the woman. The door crashed open and a gust of rock music blew in a boy and girl about twenty years old. Their dirty clothes exploded across the laundromat floor. Giggling and cracking jokes, they hurled their laundry into machines and splashed soap powder in all directions. On his black turtleneck sweater, the boy wore a yellow plastic button six inches across reading "To hell with everybody." Their antics and the insistant beat of the rock songs from their radio drowned out the romantic melodies struggling from the woman's little radio. She glared at them until they should have disintegrated before her eyes, but they didn't notice her existence.

T.C. thought it a pity that those two had come in and ruined everything for the lady. All she was doing was sitting there, crocheting and listening to her radio, and she was probably afraid to complain because they might beat her up.

When their clothes were washed, T.C. ran over to the washing machine, hurled them into a wire cart, and drove them sixty miles an hour across the laundromat to the wall of dryers. She threw open the glass-windowed door of one of the dryers and dumped the wet clothes into its cavernous mouth. The clothes whirled around, slapping against the spinning, perforated barrel.

Suddenly she realized that Caper had peeled off his shirt

and dropped it on the floor and was struggling with his jeans. By the time she got to him, he had them unzipped.

"What are you doing?"

He gestured that he wanted to put them in one of the washing machines.

T.C. shook her head. She was aware that the woman and the two jerks with the blaring radio were watching. She guided his arms back into the shirtsleeves, talking to him all the while. "We'll wash these another time," she explained. "Come on, be a good kid. Put them back on."

She hardly had him calmed down when the door opened with a crash and a man in a motorized wheelchair putt-putted into the laundromat, a cardboard carton overflowing with soiled clothes on his lap. Caper let out a holler and, shirt half-off and jeans still unzipped, hid behind T.C.

It wasn't Caper's stepfather any more than the man of the street had been, but T.C. had to go through the whole routine again, trying to make Caper understand. How many men in wheelchairs could there be in San Francisco? And Caper had to run into half of them in one morning, when she was having a hard enough time trying to keep him from freaking out. It was her kind of luck. Probably, when they left the laundromat, they would walk into a parade of men riding in wheelchairs.

By the time T.C. and Caper returned to the excavations with their clean clothes, it was after lunchtime. She heard the noon whistles blowing around town. They stopped in a bakery and bought some day-old doughnuts, and got an extra one for Moss. He had a weakness for doughnuts; if he got fifteen cents ahead he went to this particular doughnut shop on Mission for one of their old-fashioned donuts. If he scrounged a quarter, he was like a kid, because then he could afford a jelly-filled one.

But she couldn't find Moss to give him his doughnut. She remembered that she hadn't seen him that morning before going to the laundromat. She let Caper have the extra doughnut.

By evening, she was scared that something had happened to the old man. He was seventy-seven, almost seventy-eight. He might have had a stroke. Or been mugged.

She asked Goff what he thought might have happened to Moss. "His things missing?"

"What do you mean?"

"You know! Did he pack up any of his stuff to take with him?"

T.C. couldn't understand what Goff was driving at. "You think he's gone for good?"

The boy shrugged. "How should I know? It's possible, ain't it? None of us think this is the greatest place in the world, do we? So maybe he decided to split."

"But . . ."

"But he didn't tell you? Why should he? He don't owe you nothing. You're nothing to him."

T.C. felt stunned. "Oh, no!"

"What's wrong, T.C.? What is it?" Goff peered into her face. She looked as if she were about to throw up.

She shook her head, moving her hands in front of her like pinwheels. She couldn't coordinate her speech and her actions. It almost looked as if she were mimicking Caper. At last, the words burst like a bubble from her lips: "My thirty dollars!"

"You didn't give it to him?"

"He hid it for me!"

"Damn."

"Do you think . . .?"

Goff folded his arms. "What do *you* think?"

Without answering, T.C. headed straight toward the back wall of what had been Moss's cubicle. Yes, some of his things were missing. A little mirror that had been propped up on a kind of shelf, some of the rags from his bed, and a shopping bag that he carried his possessions around in: They had all vanished.

T.C. groped along the wall for those loose bricks. "I shouldn't have trusted him," she groaned. "I was a stupid fool. An idiot!"

She skinned her hands on the rough bricks and broke a nail trying to pry a brick loose from the wall.

"I'm never going to find the right place! That's what he counted on. Why did I do it?"

Goff stood behind her, like a guest at a funeral. "Maybe he didn't take your money, T.C. Maybe we're jumping to, ah, whatchamacallems."

"Conclusions. Yeah, maybe."

Like a blind girl feeling her way along a prison wall, T.C. groped with both hands over the jagged, broken brick surface. Finally a brick shifted in place when she touched it, and she eased it free and then pulled out the one next to it. She handed the bricks to Goff and reached into the hole. Her hand vanished in the darkness, as blindly she felt along the bottom, the sides, even the top. Goff found a book of matches in his jeans and handed them to her. She knew, even before she lit the match, what she would see.

"It's gone!" she wailed. "My money is gone! That old bum ran off with my money!"

Drops like fake diamonds smashed on the fallen bricks

heaped in front of the subterranean room in which T.C. sat with Goff and Caper. It had been raining for at least two hours with no indication that it would stop before dark. She stared at the drops shattering on the rubble and bouncing back into the gray air, fragments of themselves. She could think of nothing to do but watch those drops committing suicide.

It didn't matter if it rained all night and day tomorrow. It could rain forty days and forty nights; she didn't care. Let the flood come. There was nothing for her to do but wait for the waters to carry her away.

Goff tried to cheer her up, but his efforts at jokes were almost as painful as his attempts to convince her that everything would be okay. She knew that nothing was going to be okay.

"So Moss proved that he was a louse and ran off with your grubstake," he kept telling her. "That ain't no reason to roll over and play dead. You're a smart kid, T.C. I got faith in you."

But she didn't have faith in herself. She had to face it: everything that she had done since taking Caper away from Berkeley had been a mistake. A disaster was what it amounted to. She had thought that *she* could be responsible for Caper? Ha! She couldn't even take care of herself.

She was furious at herself. That was the worst of it: There was nobody to blame. Sure, that creep the first night had tried to put something over on her, and Moss had been a hypocrite and a thief, but she should have been able to see through them. She had thought that she was so smart, so shrewd at judging people. Caper could have done a better job.

She wanted to strike out at herself, to punish herself, but nothing that she could do would bring back the lost thirty bucks. She had a few dollars and some change in her jeans pocket, but how long would that last? Then what would she do? Give up and go home? Lose Caper forever? Watch him be sent away, to some orphanage or foster home, or, worse, be returned to his mother and stepfather?

"Don't be afraid, T.C. I'll find us a place to live, a better one than this. And I'll get us food and everything. I promise."

She raised her eyes from the contemplation of a puddle to Goff's dirty, pimple-dotted, big-eared face. Slowly, she focused on what he was trying to tell her.

"You?" She tried to find in his face, in his eyes, some sense of what he had said. "Why? Why should you bother about us? What are we to you?"

"I don't know. I care about you and Caper, that's all. Like you're my brother and sister or something. Don't laugh at me. I ain't no good at words. It's just a feeling I got, that's all."

Was he sincere? Or was he another of them, one of those rats who pretended to be your friend and then double-crossed you? How could she tell? She didn't have a very good track record at deciphering people's intentions.

Street smarts, Goff had said. That was what she needed, if she was going to live in this world. How was she going to get them? When would she learn how to see through the phonies and liars?

She had wanted to live "real life," but "real life" wasn't like a movie. It didn't have a beginning, a middle, or an end. It was like what her teacher, Mr. Kaufman, had said about walking: Walking is just falling, only each step catches you before you land on your face. Real life was falling on your face and then getting up again. Well, could she do it? Could she get up on her feet again?

"What about it, huh? Can't we three sort of stick together? You and me and Caper? Why can't we, T.C.?"

"I don't know."

T.C. sat, hypnotized by the falling rain, by the jagged bricks and broken pieces of concrete slowly submerging in the puddles and rivers of mud. It was easier to watch the rain and the puddles than to make a decision about what she should do next.

"Hey, listen! I won't run off with anything of yours, if that's what you're thinking, T.C. You can trust me!" Goff crouched close to her, his hands on her knees. "I'll prove it to you. I'll tell you something I never told nobody else. Not since I been out on my own. Goff ain't my real name. You know what my name is? Irving Goffman! Ain't that crappy? It makes me want to puke. So I always call myself Goff, even if it ain't my real name."

"If that's what you call yourself, then it is your name."

"Yeah. I guess so."

"Goff? Did you mean what you said? That you can find us another place to live? And food, and everything? Do you think you can?"

"Why not? Ain't I been takin' care of myself for a year, almost? I know lots of tricks. You'd be surprised."

"Why did you leave home? Why didn't you stay with your family in San Jose?"

"Mainly, see, because I don't got one—a family. I lived with my old man in a trailer, and we didn't get along so good."

"It's none of my business. I shouldn't have asked."

"No, that's okay. It don't embarrass me to talk about it. My mom ran away when I was three or four. But I didn't see a lot of her before that. My dad says she was a tramp. I don't know. I can't remember her too good. She was pretty. I know that because I used to have a picture of her. She had curly yellow hair. But one night when he was pickled, my old man tore it up. She smelled good, too. Must have been perfume, or something, but that's my best memory of her, how she smelled.

"My old man was okay most of the time, but when he got drunk, look out! That got to be just above every weekend. He'd bring home some chick, and I'd have to go out someplace, because the trailer was so little. If I came back too soon, he'd get mad and beat me up. And the chick would yell and scream, sometimes at him for hitting me and sometimes at me. Half the time, I couldn't tell who was hittin' or screamin' at who. It was a pain in the ass."

"So you ran away?"

"I walked out, that's all. I left one day and kept on goin'."

"How do you live?"

"How does *any*body live? I steal. Grown-ups do it, only they call it business, right? I figure I'm more honest than they are, 'cause I call it by its right name."

"But didn't it make you feel bad, leaving home—even if it was a trailer?"

"Hell, no. He was always telling me to get my rump out of his life, so I did."

T.C. shook her head. "I don't understand them."

"Who?"

"Adults. Why do they have kids, if they don't like us or want us?"

"Sometimes, they do want us, I guess. But they got other things on their minds, you know? And sometimes kids sort of happen, without any invitation. My father, he wasn't mean. He just couldn't be bothered. He wanted to have his life, and there I was screwing it up for him. So when he got drunk, he took it out on me. He's probably still gettin' drunk, but at least I ain't there anymore."

They both looked up at the same time and saw Caper crawling on his hands and knees through the rain, splashing in the puddles and brick-red mud.

"Oh, no!" T.C. jumped up and started shouting at Caper. Goff took her hand and pulled her back under the shelter of the concrete overhang.

"Relax. It ain't gonna hurt if he gets wet. You're his sister, not his mother."

"No. Not really. I'm not his sister. We're not related at all."

"Then what are you?"

Slowly, finding it surprisingly difficult, T.C. told Goff the true story of her relationship with Caper. Even Goff, who prided himself on his experience, opened his eyes a little wider when she described how Caper had been treated by his mother and stepfather, and the condition he'd been in the day she took him away.

"No wonder he's like that. It's a miracle he ain't worse. You did a good thing, T.C., and I don't give a damn what anybody else says."

"Really?"

She smiled at Goff. It was the first word of encouragement that anybody had offered her since she had run away. It felt good to hear somebody tell her that she was right.

"Sure. You have to do what you think is right. Screw everybody else. That's what I believe."

Soaking wet, smearing the reddish mud over his arms and legs and face, Caper stumbled into the shelter of the old brick basement overhang. Through the caked mud he grinned happily. Then, abruptly, he froze and looked at T.C. Both T.C. and Goff could see that Caper was waiting to find out if he was going to be punished.

"It doesn't matter!" said T.C.

She reached over and wiped off his face.

"I'm not mad," she said. "But I don't want you to catch cold."

Rain water dripping from his hair over his streaked face, the boy gazed into T.C.'s eyes and saw that he had nothing to fear. She understood the relief he was feeling and wanted to cry. He had been afraid of her. After all that they had survived together, after what she had tried to do for him, he had been unsure what her reaction would be. How deep the hurts in him must be, far deeper than the cigarette burns and the bruises.

With Goff's help, T.C. undressed Caper and put him into the sleeping bag.

"I can't get over it," said Goff. "That he ain't your brother. You're good with him, real good. I would've swore he must be your brother."

"You're good with him, too."

"Hell, I'm a boy, ain't I? Him and me, we got things in common. But you . . ."

"I'm only a girl."

Goff shrugged. "I didn't say that."

"Never mind. Tell me how we're going to live. *That's* what I want to know."

Goff stayed all night with Caper and T.C. Together, they listened to the rain beating on the pavement above their heads and splashing in the puddles in the excavated building site beyond their niches. Eventually, they slept, and when they woke, the clouds skidding across the slippery blue sky signaled that the storm was finished.

"Trust me," said Goff.

And, for some unknown reason, T.C. did.

She didn't want to risk trust, or love, or any other emotion again; she was tired of being disappointed and hurt. But once again she fell into the trap.

At least this time it wasn't an adult. This time she was putting her faith in another kid.

Most, if not all, adults turned out to be betrayers. It didn't hurt as much when a kid did you dirt. At least, this was what she told herself when she watched Goff hike across the muddy excavations, hopping from wet brick to wet brick. He said he'd find them a place to go, but if he didn't, he would be no worse than an adult, and with more excuse. After all, he was only fourteen. And a runaway at that.

9

Using clean rain water that had collected in an accidentally formed brick and concrete basin in the rubble, T.C. washed out Caper's dirty clothes and draped them over pieces of wall to dry in the sun. While she was at it, she washed some of her own underwear and socks. They couldn't afford to go to the laundromat again.

Goff is going to come back, she promised herself, and tell us that he's found a wonderful place, a secret little house where we'll live like real people. And nobody will bother us. Everything will be good again.

Again? When had it been good?

She shook herself into the less dazzling world of reality. Fairy tales didn't happen in real life. People didn't live happily ever after in Berkeley and San Francisco, any more than in San Jose. That happened only in the make-believe world inhabited by Snow White and Cinderella and the three little pigs.

It seemed as if she had lived for years among these ruins in the heart of San Francisco. She was sick of the dirt, of not being able to bathe properly, of being either too hot or too cold, of being hungry and thirsty. So many of the comforts of life that she had taken for granted were denied her. She hadn't thought that she would miss them, but she did.

She missed the commune's old ant heap, too; the two houses with their high-ceilinged, crowded rooms, the connecting bridge, the vegetable garden and chickens, even the sound of the basketball on the blacktop in the backyard. She thought nostalgically of her father's collection of bolts and nuts, of the whole wheat bread and granola bars that Malvina produced every week. She missed the other kids, even Kevin and Jack. She could almost imagine herself there, among them again.

T.C. stared at the funnel-shaped tracks Goff's feet had left in the now-drying red mud and thought that he was never coming back.

Caper began his wordless but insistent complaining about hunger. T.C. nodded and counted her money. She gestured for him to wait in the cubicle while she went out to see what she could buy. Dragging one foot after the other, she crossed the rubble and mud, climbed the sides of the excavation, and then hiked along the drying city pavements to the nearest market.

In the store, she trudged up and down the aisles trying to decide what to buy. The air-conditioned market was bitterly cold; when she passed between frozen food cases, goosebumps rose on her skin. She knew that she had to shop wisely. Her last two dollars and seventy cents were at stake.

She craved milk. It had been days since she had had any. Setting one quart in her basket, she moved on, past the pet food aisle (with its huge four-color pictures of well-fed cats and dogs) and the aisle piled high with potato chips and

Doritos to the produce department. They needed fruit. A couple of apples, maybe. And some kind of protein food. She knew from school that protein was important. Finally she decided on a hunk of Monterey jack cheese.

Carefully totaling up the prices and counting the money in her fist, T.C. maneuvered through the store and steered her cart up to the checkout. Paying for these few items with her last money, she thought, from now on, their lives would depend on either luck or the intervention of the gods, neither of which she had much reason to believe in.

The brown paper bag with her purchases cradled like a baby in her arms, T.C. hiked back to the excavations. She turned a wrong corner and went around several blocks that she didn't remember. She discovered a line of old men and seedy-looking young people waiting for some place to open. The sign on the door said "Plasma Center." She read the poster in the unwashed plate-glass window. "Cash for blood! Ten dollars for each donation of plasma." Ten dollars was a lot of money.

She looked at the people waiting for the door to open. The old men were propped like scarecrows against the wall, in old clothes and worn shoes, gray and white stubble on their unshaven cheeks and wine bottles and beer cans ill-concealed in crumpled paper sacks. Scattered among them were a few teenagers with long, greasy hair, patched jeans, dirt-caked bare feet, vague expressions on gaunt faces. A few other people, neither young nor old, more or less clean but poor. A couple of young men read paperback books while they waited; T.C. guessed they were college students.

T.C. went up to the pair of college students and asked what plasma was. She directed the question to the blond one with little mustache and a T-shirt that proclaimed the necessity to "Save the Whales."

"Is it like blood?"

He lowered his book, a finger marking his place. "It's the white part of the blood." He looked amused by her question. "You want to know what it's like in there?" He jerked his thumb toward the door. "What they do to you?"

T.C. nodded.

"Okay. They strap you in a big chair and put a needle in your arm and take out the whole blood. It drips into a plastic bag. Then they separate it in a centrifuge and put the red cells back into you. They sell the white stuff to companies that make serums and medicines out of it."

"You understand that?" asked the other college guy, the one with the little beard and turtleneck sweater.

"Sure. But do they really pay ten dollars for it?"

"Yeah." The first young man smiled, scratching the side of his nose with the edge of the paperback book in his hand. "But they wouldn't take you."

"Why not? Because I'm a girl?"

He shook his head.

"You're too young. You have to be eighteen."

"Oh." She shifted the groceries in her arms. "Thanks."

She marched on down the street, turned the corner, headed toward the excavations.

Every time she found a way to get money, she was too young. Even Goff would be too young to sell blood.

Would she, too, turn to stealing? She had succeeded at it once. Why not again?

She found Caper hiding in the sleeping bag. He had crawled in head first and twisted himself into a ball. When she tried to extricate him, he made frightened noises.

"What is it, Caper? Did somebody scare you?"

When he realized that it was her, he backed out of the sleeping bag and wrapped his skinny arms around her neck. He moved his mouth strenuously, like an opera singer over-enunciating the words of an aria. Suddenly, the sounds burst from his lips and hung there in the air, between them.

"Tee See!"

She stared at him as if he had turned into solid gold before her eyes.

"Yes, Caper! I'm T.C. That's me! You said it! Yes! You can talk! You can hear me, can't you? You know my name! You know!"

She hugged him to her, forgetting his sores, his bruises, forgetting everything but that he had actually formed the two syllables that stood for her.

"Wait till I tell Goff. You'll have to do it for him, too! Can you say anything else? Can you say your name? Caper? That's your name: Caper. Can you say it?"

But he looked frightened now, and she didn't want to push him. So she sat on the bricks, her arm around him, happier than she had been for a long, long time.

By evening, T.C. had given up hope that Goff would return. He, too, had betrayed her. At least, she consoled herself, he didn't get anything out of me.

The next time somebody told her to trust him, she knew what her comeback would be.

But Caper could talk. He had pronounced her name. It would just be a matter of helping him to gain confidence, now. She had something to live for, a goal.

She gave Caper an apple and some cheese and crackers and let him finish the last of the milk. Then she put him in the sleeping bag. He was still thin and weak, but the bruises and burns were fading. How long would it be before the memories faded, she wondered? Or were they like the scars on his body? Would he always have them? Would he ever stop waking up at night, shaking with fear? Did he trust her yet?

She had to laugh at that. Here she had decided not to trust anybody and she wanted Caper to learn to trust her. Why should he trust her? Was she better than anybody else?

Maybe he would be better off in a foster home. Maybe even in an orphanage. At least, he would always have the same bed and enough to eat and the same people around him all the time. Maybe, if she loved him, she would give him up.

T.C. squatted at the front of the small subterranean cubicle that was now hers and Caper's, and stared at the lights of the city flashing on against the darkness. An orange beacon revolved on the top of a nearby skyscraper. Red, white, and blue fragments of light blinked overhead, as planes approached and took off from the airport. Someday, she wanted to take a long trip on an airplane, to Europe or around the world, and find out if other people came up against life the way she had. Was it the same in France and China and all those places? In school they never talked about real life, about how people in different countries survived. They didn't tell you what it was really like in this country. They brainwashed you about how wonderful America was, but they didn't educate you about the bad things, too. It seemed to T.C. that it was more important to be prepared for the bad things; you can discover the nice ones for yourself.

She was trying to talk herself into giving up Caper, but she didn't want to admit defeat. "Hell," she told the darkness. "I'm only twelve!"

"Hey, what're you doin', anyway, talkin' to yourself again?"

"Goff!" She peered into the darkness. "You rat! You scared me half to death!"

She saw him, now, half-silhouetted against the checkerboard patterned lights of the Pacific Telephone Building.

"What took you so long? Where were you?"

His outline grew as he approached, and then his features swam into focus among the shadows. He was grinning, with that superior, cocky expression that used to bug her, but she was glad to see that smug, broken-toothed grin.

"Didn't you think I was coming back?"

She shook her head. She was afraid that she was going to cry and didn't want him to know that she had cared so much.

"I said I would, T.C. And I always keep my promises—I mean, if I want to, and I wanted to, this time."

She nodded toward the little hut: "Want an apple?"

"Sure. All I've had to eat all day was a banana I pinched at one of the sidewalk markets on Grant and a candy bar I picked up in Long's Drugstore."

T.C. gave him the food that she had left and told him about Caper's word. To her annoyance, he didn't seem excited by the news.

"I knew that kid was no dummy. I knew it all along."

She hid her disappointment by asking him where he had gone.

"Where didn't I go? I found some deserted houses in the outer Mission, but they're gonna be torn down pretty soon. They're boarded up. The windows're broken, they stink of piss and rats are all over the place. Then I saw some buildings out by the Fillmore, but they was just as bad, and the neighborhood is pretty rough. A dude could get knifed for walking on the wrong side of the street."

"So you never did find a place?"

"Wait a minute! Did I say that? Did I? Just give me a chance, will you? I went all the way down to the end of Van Ness and over to Ghiradelli Square and Fisherman's

Wharf. Tried to pick up some change from the tourists, but got run off by a cop. Then I cruised around the waterfront for a while. You know, by the docks and warehouses. And I found us a place, T.C. I think I found us a real good place."

Something about his voice put T.C. on her guard.

"What . . . kind of a place?"

"It's sort of a warehouse. But nice and clean."

"A warehouse."

"I didn't see no rats. Not even any rat messes."

"Fantastic."

"No kidding, T.C. It's a okay place. Has a roof and everything. Nobody ever uses those old warehouses. No ships come in anymore, so the warehouses are empty. Some of 'em have been torn down and a few've burned up, but you'd be surprised how many are sittin' there, rotting away. It's fine, T.C. No lie."

What could she say? "Okay."

"We'll go there tomorrow. It's a lot better'n this hole. And there ain't nobody else around. That's the best part: The place'll be ours."

Suddenly, T.C. was cold. She nodded and said that she was going to go to sleep. She crawled into the sleeping bag beside Caper. It was several minutes before she stopped shaking.

She heard Goff settling himself for the night, then he was quiet too. "Goff," she called, softly.

"Yeah?"

"Thanks."

"Oh, sure. That's okay, T.C."

She pressed her face into the slick fabric of the sleeping bag and closed her eyes. She managed to sleep straight through until morning.

T.C. woke up early as the pink sky slowly blossomed into blue, and lay in the warmth of the sleeping bag, thinking about the future. A transformation seemed to have occurred in her during the night; maybe her latent cowardice had surfaced. Whatever the cause, she wasn't so enthusiastic now about going away with Goff. It was too scary, moving to an unknown place, relying on a person who had been a stranger only days before. What was she letting herself and Caper in for? At least, she knew what to expect here. She was tired; she didn't want to wander anymore. She felt like a war refugee, one of those ragged scarecrows she had seen staggering among the ruins of Europe in old newsreels in her history class. She knew how they must have felt: no food, no hope, and unable to put one foot in front of the other. The exhaustion was more than physical. It was emotional, spiritual. She felt used up, like a wadded Kleenex thrown out of a car window. She wanted to stay curled up in the sleeping bag forever, and let the world fade away into nothingness.

The midmorning sun inched around the broken bricks, until it found its way to her face. She squeezed her eyes tight against the glare. Beside her, Caper slept on and on. She had never known anyone who could sleep as much as Caper. Maybe that was his way of blocking out a world he didn't know how to cope with.

Was she like him? Afraid to face the world?

She opened her eyes and stared at the rough-textured bricks near her face. A procession of ants, searching for food for their colony, trudged across the sandpaperlike red surface. She maneuvered out of the sleeping bag and shoved her feet into her shoes. She needed to think. Walking always helped her to get her thoughts together. She crawled out of the half-cave and stumbled over the rubble.

The mud left by the storm was drying. Some of the puddles were actually steaming, shrinking before her eyes.

She didn't see Goff anyplace, but she knew that he hadn't run out on them. She almost wished that he had taken off; then her decision would have been made for her.

Sometimes almost on her hands and knees, crawling among the piles of debris, other times striding across the open field, she made her way across the spaces left by the demolition crews so long ago. She might have been clambering over the exotic, broken surface of the moon. Only when she lifted her eyes to the city skyline did she remember that she was in San Francisco.

Crouching, like one of those long-tailed, skinny monkeys at the zoo, using her hands as well as her feet, she climbed a steep pile of rubble. At the top of the small mountain, she stood erect and surveyed the spectacle around her. Her gaze followed the horizon, blinking against the blue of the sky. She nearly gasped aloud when she saw a pair of booted feet extended, toes up, from beneath the rubble, a few yards below her.

Abruptly, the boots moved and a hairy head and ragged shoulders rose from behind a pile of bricks. The man leered at her, a cigar stub in his mouth. She couldn't tell how old he was, but age had nothing to do with the meanness she saw in his eyes.

T.C.'s foot shifted weight, sending several bricks clattering over the rubble. The man gestured angrily at her, curses sizzling around her ears.

T.C. jumped down from her vantage point and ran across the open field. She leaped from mound to mound, dodged unexpected holes, stumbled over loose rocks and bricks, until she reached the row of subterranean dwellings that had become the center of her world.

Only when she stopped running, flushed and sweaty, did she realize how scared she was. Although she was standing in the sun, she was trembling as violently as if she had stepped into a blizzard.

"T.C.!" Goff scrambled through the bricks toward her. "You scared me! I thought you'd run out on me—or got hurt!"

What was he saying? She stared into his dirty face. Yes, he looked as if he had been worried about her. He did care what happened to her. How strange, that he should be such a vital part of her life in such a short time. For she knew, now, that despite her doubts she was going with him. She did intend to put herself and Caper in his grubby hands.

The morning sun warmed them as they hiked over the hills toward the bay. Caper seemed to be excited, as if he understood that they were leaving behind them their transient existence and going to a home.

"It won't be long, now," Goff encouraged them. "Just a few more blocks."

"It doesn't matter."

The walk was nothing. It didn't bother T.C. at all. What concerned her was the unknown future.

Trudging half-bent, with the backpack against her narrow shoulders, T.C. saw something glinting on the curb, a bit of gold, perhaps a piece of jewelry. Crouching, she scooped it up in her hand and examined it: a single earring, a loop of pale gold with a delicate tracery like a pattern of lace on one side of its curved surface. She balanced it in her palm and studied its fragile yellow beauty. A woman had lost it and would never know where. Had she been on her way to a party or a movie? Had she missed it right away, or not until she got home that evening? How valuable was it?

T.C. couldn't tell if the earring was genuine gold or not, but it provoked an image from her past, a vague picture that slowly rose to the surface of her brain, like a fish swimming up from the depths of a murky pool.

A face: Whose was it? A pretty face, girlish, yet not a girl, laughing, holding her hair away from her head to show off a gold flower clamped to her earlobe.

Of course! It was her mother. Long ago, before they had joined the commune, T.C.'s mother had worn earrings. Why had she stopped? T.C. saw those earrings as clearly as the one in her hand. She had been only four or five, but she had loved those tiny gold flowers. The center had flipped open to reveal a tiny bit of cotton on which T.C.'s mother had put a drop of perfume each time she wore the earrings. Those earrings had seemed to be the most wonderful objects in the world to T.C. Where were they now? Did her mother have them packed away in a drawer, or had she tossed them out when they moved into the commune?

Oh, God, she missed her mother!

"What've you got? Did you find something?"

Goff waited at the corner. T.C. shook her head. "No. Nothing. Just a piece of junk." She tossed the earring into the gutter and hurried to catch up with Goff. The world was filled with little traps like that, to torment her with the past. She would have to be careful.

I am not going to be sentimental, she told herself. I am going to be tough. Goff thinks I'm just a weak girl, but I'll show him. I'm as good as any boy. Or better.

They descended a steep, narrow street between rows of gaunt frame houses, each only two or three windows wide. The houses were cluttered with small porches, steeply gabled roofs, and bay windows, with gingerbread trim around the eaves and stained glass on the front doors. They were well-cared for, with swept sidewalks and recent coats of paint.

Then, abruptly, the neighborhood changed. The houses weren't so well painted, the sidewalks and streets were adrift with litter, and weeds grew between the cracks in the pavement. On one corner, an old mom and pop grocery was boarded up. Election posters hung in tatters from its walls and fragments of newspapers were blown up against its shredded screen door. The shadows of warehouses fell across the street.

No cars were parked at the curb down here, and when a motorcycle whizzed past, both T.C. and Caper jumped. They might have been miles instead of blocks from the center of town.

They passed mutilated tires lying in the street, broken glass scattered over curb and sidewalk, a pair of long-abandoned shoes curling in the sun. T.C. had to look back, up the hill, to believe that only moments before they had been walking through a tidy, ordinary San Francisco neighborhood. From certain angles, she could see fragments of skyscrapers in the financial district or the top stories of the hotels on Nob Hill. Everything seemed at once far away and close.

The more they walked, the more the dark, naked wood of the warehouse walls closed in around them. Puddles from yesterday's rain lingered in dark corners.

"There!"

T.C. looked around, trying to decide the building Goff meant. They all appeared equally grim.

"That one! For cryin' out loud, are you blind!"

He pointed at a massive building spread out across the street like a gray whale beached in a storm; the expanse of weathered wood was broken only by a door at one end. At least five stories high, the warehouse stretched the length of the block. A row of many-paned, mostly broken windows extended along the top, like black eyes gazing down on the street. While T.C. studied the building, a shingle blew off the roof and turned a series of midair somersaults before clattering onto the street.

"Is that how we go in?"

She pointed to the mouthlike door at the far end of the dead whale's gray corpse.

"No, somebody might see us. There's another way in through the alley around the corner."

Abandoning the sunlight on their side of the street, they plunged into the shadow cast by the warehouse. The building must have been unused for many years; only faded red streaks remained of the paint that had once covered the gray wood. Boards hung loose at gawky angles, and a rusted metal sign drooped cockeyed over one of the two ground-floor windows. ". . . HNSON BROS."

"Come on." Goff led T.C. and Caper up the alley, between the warehouse and a deserted metalworks factory. A twisted bumper from a small car and a shattered automobile headlight lay in the middle of the pavement; every step seemed to kick up a bolt or a nut or a hunk of rusted metal. T.C. smiled to think what a gold mine of treasures this alley would be for her father.

On this side of the warehouse, huge sliding doors capable of opening up wide enough to allow trucks to pass through were bolted into place with enormous, rusty padlocks. Rust-colored railroad tracks let out of the doors and stopped abruptly.

"This is our door."

Goff pushed open a narrow wooden door beside the large doors and stepped over a high wooden threshold into the blackness. Behind him, T.C. and Caper hesitated, reluctant to plunge into the featureless black space.

"It's okay, T.C. I checked it out. Some of the floor's rotten, but just stay with me."

T.C. wasn't scared of rotten floorboards. She was afraid that the whole building would collapse on them. It was huge, but so aged and worn that it looked as if a strong gust of wind would start a chain reaction, with beams collapsing and walls toppling and the roof caving in and the whole place groaning and crying out in agony as it fell in on itself in a great cloud of rusty dust. But she couldn't hurt Goff's feelings. He was so proud of having discovered this place for them. So, she stored her fears in the back of her brain and, clutching Caper by the hand, stepped over the rotten threshold.

She felt Caper tug on her hand as he drew back. He didn't want to go into that darkness any more than she did. But they followed Goff down a long hallway, dimly illuminated by the windows high overhead, to a vast room that reminded T.C. of an old railroad station that she had been in once. It was lit by skylights far above, but the glass that remained in them was so dirty and caked with dust that light could penetrate only through the broken panes.

Goff led them to some wooden stairs and they climbed toward a mezzanine overlooking the vast concrete floor beyond the wooden entry that they had crossed. From above, they could see the shadowy carcasses of huge pieces of machinery, like the corpses of dinosaurs, scattered in the great chamber. The staircase swayed and groaned as they climbed to the mezzanine. T.C.'s hand groped for the wooden railing and, sliding through thick spider webs, stirred up clouds of dust.

The mezzanine fronted a row of small rooms. They must

have been offices, T.C. decided, from which the bosses could look down over the men laboring below.

Goff turned the knob on one of the glass-windowed doors, pushed and then pulled and finally gave the door a kick. The door swung open with a crash, and he gestured for T.C. and Caper to go into the room.

"I cleaned it up for you," he said.

Goff's idea of clean and T.C.'s notion of clean were not the same. As far as she could tell, no one had stirred the dust in that room for decades. Then she saw that somebody had smeared the dirt on the windows a little, and perhaps had ripped down some cobwebs and shifted some garbage to one corner. She had to admit that he had made an effort, and she was touched that he had cared enough to bother.

"Thanks," she said. "It's real nice."

That night, they slept close together in the center of the room. T.C. woke up several times, listening to the groaning of the old building. She thought that she heard footsteps on the staircase. Once, she was positive that somebody was opening the door. When she did sleep, she dreamed that they had found their way to an elegant hotel where the staff had been overjoyed to serve the famous T.C. Helprin (who was famous chiefly for being famous) and her friends, and had competed to see who could bring the most good things for them, but when the first rays of the morning sun penetrated the smudged windows, everything was the same as it had been the day before. The thick, unpainted floorboards were splintered and warped, some loose, scattered with yellowed, crumpled newspapers, rusty nails and screws, and, contrary to Goff's promise, rodent droppings.

They woke hungry.

"I'll get some food," Goff announced. "Don't worry."

T.C. was not optimistic: "I've only got eighty-six cents left."

"Who needs it? I got ways."

"Goff, what if you get caught?"

"Me, the Great Goff, get caught? You're out of your skull!"

T.C. shifted her eighty-six cents from one hand to the other. "Don't you want to take this, just in case?"

"Hell, no. Be back in a flash!"

He was out of the room and crashing down the rickety stairs before she could say anything else.

Goff lived up to his boast. He brought back, hidden on various parts of his body, a package of sliced salami, some cheese, a couple of small cans of apple juice, Oreo cookies, and a Hostess apple turnover.

While Goff had been rounding up breakfast, T.C. had explored the warehouse. In a nest of cobwebs in an office a few doors down the mezzanine, she discovered an ancient broom, which she put to use. She swept everything that she could reach and then took one of Caper's T-shirts and scrubbed at the window. She didn't expect Goff to notice any difference, and he didn't.

They sat on the floor and divided the salami and cheese and Oreos, passing around the pop-top cans of apple juice while they ate. Maybe, thought T.C., they would make out okay. It was possible, she decided, as she watched Goff and Caper munching on fistfuls of Oreos, that their luck was changing.

So far, running away had been disappointing. Not just because people had lied and robbed her and would have done worse if given half a chance. Not even because she had found life on her own to be so hard. No, the real disappointment was that running away had turned out to be so commonplace. From the security of home, the prospect had seemed exciting and daring, but, despite the frightening moments, it had been pretty boring.

Still, she was on her own, wasn't she? Her own boss. She could clean out this place, or not, as she chose; she could gobble up the Oreos or save some for later, and no adult would scold or praise her, whichever she did. The experience of being responsible for herself was new enough to be exhilarating, and, now that she had begun to feel less afraid of the future, some of her old self-confidence returned.

Laughing, teasing each other, rolling on the rough wooden floor, they finished off the Oreos and divided the sugar-coated apple turnover. Warm sunlight fell in shafts through the windows, catching particles of dust like fragments of gold in the air. A spider labored on a web in a corner above the door, preparing diligently for her dinner.

The trio had finished their breakfast sometime near twelve. After dozing languidly for a couple of hours in the warmth of the fly-buzzing afternoon, they began to feel hungry again. They tried to ignore the message of their stomachs, but finally Goff sat up and announced that he would go out on another foraging expedition.

"I wish you didn't have to steal," said T.C. "It's not right."

"Starving ain't right, neither."

"You might get caught."

"Ah," he said, with an impish grin. "That's a better reason, if you're tryin' to talk me out of payin' one of my visits to the supermarket, but you're forgettin' one thing."

"What's that?"

"Nobody ever catches the Great Goff!"

His smirk was so ridiculous that she had to laugh at him as he sauntered out the door.

While he was gone, she rearranged their possessions in the small room, explored the other offices again, dragged back two broken chairs and a small table, which she cleaned off with Caper's all-purpose T-shirt, and found the lavatory. When she tried the faucet, the pipe moaned and a dead insect fell into the dusty basin. The water had been turned off long ago.

"Damn!" More than anything else, T.C. hated being dirty. Her most frequent fantasy was a long luxurious bath, with all the hot water she wanted.

Each day, Goff made one or two forays into the world and returned laden with supplies. Whatever the weather, he wore his bulky, well-padded jacket. From its depths he could produce an astonishing quantity of goods, ranging from a quart of milk or a couple of cans of Coke to several bananas and half a dozen oranges to a full, uncut Italian salami. Whatever T.C. requested, he provided, including a roll of paper towels, toilet tissue, soap, toothpaste, toothbrushes, even vitamin pills. She had to admit that he was talented.

"When you grow up, you should work for the CIA or somebody."

"Nah, I wouldn't want to do that. I'd have to go to college."

"Then what do you want to do?"

"Heck, I don't know. Never thought about it. Keep on going the way I am, I guess."

"But . . ." T.C. couldn't imagine living this way forever. "Don't you have any ambition?"

"No. Why should I?"

T.C. let the subject drop, but she could imagine Goff in a few years, lined up with the winos and bums, waiting for the Plasma Center to open.

How could she warn Goff of the dangers of this nomad's existence? He did so much for them. He really cared about Caper and her, she knew. And she cared about him. That was the trouble.

He was always trying to surprise them, to brighten their lives with his jokes and foolishness and, sometimes, with unexpected little presents. Like the bubbles.

One day, after they had been living in the warehouse about a week, Goff finished depositing his collection of food on the table and then waved his arms over his head, gesturing like a magician that he had once seen on television, and reached again into his jacket and produced one additional object: a pink plastic bottle with a couple of wire wands attached to its sides. A magic bubble set!

"I'm gonna teach Caper how to blow bubbles!" he informed T.C. "I'll bet he ain't never blown a single bubble in his life."

With elaborate ritual, Goff unscrewed the cap from the bottle, took one of the wands, dunked it into the soapy liquid, and held it in front of Caper's face. The younger boy stared at the strange object, but did nothing.

"Blow! Go ahead, kid, blow!" Nothing. "See, like this!"

Goff puffed out his cheeks and puckered his lips and blew into the trembling translucent liquid caught on the wire loop. The liquid stretched, broke away from the wire, and burst free into the air, a shiny, buoyant pink bubble.

Caper's eyes grew huge and his mouth dropped open and he actually crowed with delight. The bubble hovered in the air before him, reflecting the light from the window, and then slowly sank to the floor, where it burst, leaving a small damp spot on the thirsty wood.

"Uhhhh!"

Caper turned from Goff to T.C. and then stared, heartbroken, at the place where the bubble had been.

"Don't worry, kid," announced Goff. "The Great Goff will continue to amaze and delight you." He dunked the wire wand, blew out another bubble, then dunked it again and again, until half a dozen pink orbs of varying sizes were floating in front of Caper's face. "Bubbles to the left of you, bubbles to the right of you, bubbles, bubbles, bubbles!"

He surrounded Caper with bubbles; he caught the bubbles on the wire loop and carried them right to Caper's nose. He blew on the bubbles and made them rise on his breath almost to the ceiling before they burst.

"Here, T.C. You blow bubbles for a while. I'm getting dizzy."

Feeling silly, yet enjoying herself more than she would admit, T.C. dunked the wire wand and blew more bubbles to amuse Caper. At first, she blew too hard; it had been so long since she had played at what she considered a babyish game. But then she got the hang of it, and had as many bubbles floating through the air as Goff had produced.

"Give him the other wand, T.C. Let him try it now."

T.C. dunked the second wire wand into the solution and held it up in front of Caper. He stared at it for a moment, then, with a look of extreme concentration on his face, blew. Like T.C., his first puff was more calculated to blow down one of the three little pigs' houses than to create a bubble, but his second try released a series of tiny bubbles. He laughed gleefully, and his next attempt produced a huge, glittering pink bubble that rose straight up toward the sky.

For the first time, Caper seemed like an ordinary boy, not an abused child, not a scared, battered, hungry orphan on the run, but any nine-year-old boy having some fun with his friends.

They blew bubbles all afternoon.

"More!" he cried, when Goff started to put away the bottle of liquid soap. "More!"

His second word! T.C. and Goff looked at each other with silent pride and satisfaction.

"Okay, kid," said Goff. "You can blow bubbles all night, if you want to. Who gives a damn? We can do what we please, and that includes blowing bubbles!"

A few days later, the biggest surprise yet appeared from beneath Goff's magic jacket.

Instead of ceremonially unloading his jacket's contents onto the table as he usually did, Goff strode over to Caper, who was sitting in the corner on the floor, playing with the empty bubble solution bottle. He turned the boy's head and pointed to a bulge inside his jacket.

"I've got a present for you," he told Caper, again pointing with one hand to something that he had confined inside his jacket.

Eagerly, Caper held up the pink plastic bottle.

"No, not more bubbles. Something better than bubbles, Caper."

He pronounced the words carefully. Caper gave no indication that he understood, but he jumped back with a combination of fear and excitement when he saw the bulge in Goff's jacket move.

"Goff, what *is* it?" asked T.C. "What do you have under there?"

"Something for the kid."

The unseen creature wriggled and twitched beneath the filthy imitation leather jacket, sending Goff into convulsions of laughter.

"It tickles! Geez, you two, can't you guess what it is? What a pair of dumbbells!"

A tiny brown tail slipped from beneath the zippered jacket.

"A dog!" T.C. knelt in front of Goff. "You brought Caper a puppy!"

Caper understood, now, that an animal was hiding under Goff's jacket and that the animal was for him. Grinning and wriggling as much as the puppy sliding out of the jacket, he reached for it, drew back, shook his hands with excitement, reached out again. At last, with great daring, he stroked the fully exposed, fur-covered wormlike tail.

"Unnnh!"

Goff could restrain neither the puppy nor his own eagerness any longer, and with one deft motion he unzipped the jacket and let the puppy fall onto Caper's lap.

"Watch out!" cried T.C., but Caper already had the tiny brown animal cradled in his arms.

The boy held the puppy up to his face, rubbing its fur against his cheek. He kissed it on the nose and, when it licked his mouth and chin with its pink tongue, gurgled with joy.

T.C. and Goff knelt beside Caper, watching him let the puppy crawl over his head and shoulders. T.C. had never seen Caper so happy.

"Unnnh!" said Caper happily. "Mine!"

T.C. sat forward, and stared at Caper.

"*Mine*!" he repeated, firmly.

His third word!

"Yes, Caper." T.C. sighed. "Yours. The puppy is yours."

"Mine."

The puppy squeaked and Caper made noises at it, and they had their own private conversation, interspersed with that one word, "Mine." They rolled on the floor together, and T.C. was afraid that Caper might hurt the puppy, but then she saw that he cradled it in his hands, gently lifting it into the air, tickling it, stroking it, experiencing its softness, its smallness, its wonderful vulnerability. She didn't have to worry about Caper harming the pup.

"Goff," she whispered. "That's the nicest thing I've ever seen anybody do, bringing that dog to Caper."

"Hell," said Goff. "It's only a mutt." But he grinned with pride and satisfaction.

Neither of them thought now about the complications that a pet would add to their existence, but even if they had, they wouldn't have cared.

T.C. and Caper took the puppy to a small hillside park half a dozen blocks away, overlooking the bay and the roofs of the narrow Victorian houses marching up and down the straight streets. The pup hurtled through the grass, running so fast down the steep lawn that it catapulted head over paws, a fuzzy brown ball rolling down the hill. Caper dashed after it, scooped it up with both hands, and rubbed it against his face, as if kissing better any hurts it might have suffered. They played in the park for more than an hour every day.

Sometimes, they explored the neighborhoods adjacent to the old warehouse district. Occasionally, Goff went with them, but he was an independent person, and, as much as he liked T.C. and Caper, he needed to spend time away from them. Sometimes, he told T.C. where he went, often he didn't. But he never failed to bring something back to eat, even if it was only candy bars. He never told T.C. precisely how or where he acquired the stuff, and she didn't ask.

Now, Goff brought back dog food, as well, but he met this added responsibility with good humor. After all, *he* had dropped the pup into their laps.

When T.C. suggested that they should get jobs, Goff ridiculed the idea. Nobody would hire them, he said. They were only kids. Maybe he could get a job delivering papers, but you only earned chicken feed at jobs like that. He didn't want to waste his time in the early morning, before it was even light, folding Chronicles and slipping rubber bands around 'em. And how the devil could he deliver the things? He didn't even have a bike. No, they didn't need jobs. He'd see that they got by okay, just as they were. Wasn't he the Great Goff?

A couple of days later, Goff leaped into the room, startling Caper and sending the pup scampering, and announced that they were going to the beach. The dog, too.

"We gotta get this kid out this room. He needs fresh air."

"We go to the park, sometimes."

"Ain't enough. We're gonna go run on the sand, let the pup chase sea gulls or whatever they are: the whole trip. And buy ourselves some hot doggies. We're gonna have ourselves a real day—you see if we don't!"

T.C. shrugged. She wasn't going to argue. It sounded like fun. But she hoped they wouldn't be too tired to enjoy it when they got there.

"It's a long walk to Ocean Beach."

"We ain't walkin'. We're goin' in style, on the bus!" She looked at him with disbelief, and he answered the unspoken question: "I've got enough money, don't worry."

"But . . . we can't take animals on the bus, not without a cage, or something."

"You leave that to the Great Goff."

"Well, okay," said T.C., doubtfully. "But shouldn't we take something to eat for lunch?"

"I *told* you, I'm gonna *buy* us lunch. You sure are hard to get through to. What's your brain made out of, concrete?"

They had to transfer twice to get across San Francisco from the bay side to Ocean Beach, but they all enjoyed the ride, except possibly the dog, which traveled hidden beneath Goff's jacket. Caper kept looking anxiously at the bulge over Goff's chest, but when he was satisfied that his puppy was safe, he let himself take in the spectacle beyond the bus' wide windows. As far as T.C. knew, this was the first time Caper had ever ridden a city bus.

The sun vanished behind a silver-gray haze, and suddenly, ahead of the bus stretched the Pacific Ocean, a line of dark green hovering between the misty sky and the solid earth.

As soon as they climbed down from the bus, they smelled the difference in the air. Caper froze on the pavement beside the muni coach, staring across the wide, almost empty, parking lot to the great gray retaining wall and the ocean beyond.

Waves broke on the beach. The ocean breeze swept up over the damp sand, biting the flesh of their faces and chilling them through their clothing, and the mist refreshed their skin. Goff dropped the pup on the beach and they watched it turn in excited circles, like a dancer trying to remember his steps, and then take off down the slope toward the water. Caper let out a cry of horror, as if he thought the waves would swallow his pet.

"Go after him, Caper!" T.C. urged. "Go play with him."

Caper looked up at her, and she motioned toward the water. His expression changed as he realized that it was *okay* to run here and play with his pup. He galloped down the slope, leaving rough-edged prints in the damp sand,

and watched his pet challenging the wavelets lapping at the beach. The tiny dog yipped and growled shrilly, as the pintsized waves broke on the shore, inches away from his nose. Then he attacked too fiercely, inhaled saltwater, and leaped backward with a sneeze.

T.C. and Goff, standing up the beach a few yards, laughed.

"You were right, Goff. This *is* good for both of them."

T.C. hadn't been to Ocean Beach for years. She was fascinated by the birds everywhere, especially the seagulls covering the huge gray rocks far out in the water.

"Look, T.C.," Goff told her. "Seals! Over there—on that side of the rocks."

She looked where Goff pointed, and then glanced at him again. His face radiated excitement like a spotlight.

"Goff, have you ever been here before?"

He shook his head.

"I ain't never even seen the ocean before. Ain't it somethin'? Ain't it the biggest thing you ever saw in your life?"

A couple of joggers in sweat suits plodded past, shouting friendly greetings, and Goff waved good-naturedly. This was a wonderful treat, but one thought nagged at T.C. "Goff, where'd you get the money for all this?"

"Oh, I got it, don't worry about it."

And he ran off to join Caper and the pup at the water's edge.

Far up the beach, where the waves were higher, crashing around the jagged rocks and breaking in great white lacy curtains on the sandy slope, half a dozen men pulled black rubber costumes over swimming suits and dragged surfboards out into the blue-green water. T.C. didn't understand how they could bear to dive into that icy ocean, but she watched them paddle far out toward the horizon and try to ride their boards on the waves. They were all dumped into the water well before the beach.

"Come on!" shouted Goff. "Let's go get something to eat. All this fresh air is making my stomach growl!"

It was true, the salt spray or the half-medicinal smell of the kelp washed up on the beach or maybe the excitement did give them roaring appetites.

They left the beach, Caper carrying his pup, and hiked up the road beside the huge, curving seawall, following the shape of the shore until they reached several angular buildings clinging to the rocks. A sign identified one of them as the Cliff House Restaurant.

"We can't eat there!" T.C. gasped. "It's too expensive. They wouldn't let us in, anyway."

Goff laughed, stroking the pup in Caper's arms.

"I didn't say we was gonna eat there, did I?" He pointed up the road, past a bus load of tourists. "That's where we're getting lunch."

A hot dog stand!

Sitting on a bench beside the rough-textured concrete seawall, they munched on foot-long hot dogs and French fries and watched the gulls hopping on the rocks below. T.C. tried to point out the seals to Caper, but he didn't seem to understand what she was talking about. He preferred feeding half of his frankfurter to the pup.

Goff bought him a second hot dog and told him to keep most of it for himself.

"Mine," said Caper.

"Yeah," Goff affirmed. "Yours."

But Caper gave part of it to his pup, anyway.

T.C. still looked troubled. "This is wonderful, Goff. But how did you get the money?"

"I earned it," he said, looking out at the Pacific Ocean. "I did a little job, okay? So don't worry." He jerked his fist toward the beach. "Come on, let's go run on the sand."

New tour buses pulled up in front of the Cliff House and disgored brightly garbed middle-aged men and women with instamatic cameras growing in front of their faces. T.C. and Goff led Caper down the road to the beach.

"Your trouble, T.C.," Goff shouted at her, as they jogged across the sand, "is that you worry too much."

T.C. grabbed Goff's arm and pulled him around so that he faced her. They stood inches apart on the damp sand.

"Maybe I *should* worry. Goff, don't lie to me. How did you get the money for today?"

"Okay, you win. I snatched a old lady's purse. So what? There wasn't much in it."

T.C. stared at him.

"You did, didn't you? You're not joking. You really did steal an old lady's purse."

"Sure, wanta make somethin' of it?" He grinned, but T.C. refused to be swayed by his tattered charm. "Listen, girl, I didn't do nothin' that plenty of other guys don't do."

"Don't you see, Goff? That ruins everything. You told me you didn't steal from people, just stores. Not from individuals who might suffer." T.C. gripped his arm firmly. "Did you hurt her? Did you knock her down and kick her? Tell me the truth, Goff. Did you break her legs or kick her in the teeth? How did you make that old woman give up her purse?"

"No! You're not fair, T.C. I didn't hurt her, I swear it. I grabbed it out of her hands and ran. That's all. She only had seven bucks in it. And some change. Not even a credit card or nothin'. I didn't knock her down. I wouldn't do that, T.C."

"I feel like I ought to vomit up that hot dog. Don't you see, Goff? The whole day, it's no good, now."

"It was okay until you knew, wasn't it? What difference does it make?"

"It does, that's all!"

She looked around for Caper and the pup and realized that they weren't there.

"Caper! Goff—where's Caper?"

He shook his head. "What? I don't know. Isn't he around here someplace?"

"Around here someplace? What're you talking about? I'm responsible for him."

"Relax. How far could he go? The ocean's on one side and the freeway on the other."

"You think that's funny? Goff, if anything happens to him—"

T.C. ran across the beach, calling Caper. A few people looked up at the twelve-year-old girl waving her arms and shouting, but nobody paid much attention. It was her problem, whatever it was. It didn't concern them.

"Caper!" Oh, God, she thought, where is he? He can't be drowned, he can't be!

She ran along the edge of the water, looking for footprints, for some sign that he had passed this way.

No, maybe he had gone the other direction, toward the freeway. Maybe he had tried to cross that wide road, looking for the bus stop. Maybe the pup had run away and he had chased it out into the traffic. What if they had run in front of one of those tour buses?

She tried to think: Had she heard any brakes squealing? She turned in a circle, not knowing which way to go. "I'll do *any*thing, if he's not hurt!" she yelled, not knowing who or what she was talking to, just promising the ocean, the sky, the world. "Anything!"

"You shouldn't oughta say things you don't mean."

T.C. whirled around. There was Goff, with the pup in one arm and leading Caper with his other hand. "They just went off exploring together."

T.C. fell to her knees on the damp sand, hugging Caper. "You found him!"

"Of course, girl. Did you forget? I'm the Great Goff!"

10

"Unnh, unnh!"

Caper crawled on his hands and knees, pushing a scrap of hamburger toward the long-tongued puppy. He insisted on sharing his food with his pet. The dog had spurned such human delights as marshmallows and potato chips, but he gobbled up the hunk of greasy hamburger, even licking the mustard from the floor.

They had never named the animal. T.C. felt that, since the dog belonged to Caper, he should name it, but he had uttered nothing sounding like a name, so the dog remained "Puppy" or "It."

It was definitely a mutt, part golden retriever, part an undefined terrier, with maybe a bit of poodle someplace in its lineage. The combination was not unpleasing, but as the beast grew it took on a decided comic aspect. He flopped around the room like a young deer, tripping on his own legs, crashing into walls, and sometimes collapsing in a brown and gray heap.

They all loved him excessively.

The weather grew colder. T.C. asked Goff what they would do when winter hit them in earnest. He only laughed.

"I'll take care of you and the kid," he said. "I'll cut my hand off to do it, if I gotta."

"You don't have to cut off your hand," said T.C.

The next day, Goff went out. After he left, T.C. and Caper walked the few blocks to Fisherman's Wharf. Here, within sight of abandoned docks and warehouses, they strolled past expensive restaurants, peered into crowded souvenir shops, and watched tourists buying three-dollar crab cocktails at sidewalk stalls. T.C. was surprised there were so many tourists wandering around in the middle of November.

T.C. and Caper worked up a good appetite and returned to the warehouse expecting to find Goff waiting with his newest acquisitions.

He wasn't there.

T.C. let Caper finish the crackers and cheese that she found in their food box. They waited until nightfall, but Goff never showed up.

That night, T.C. and Caper crawled into their sleeping bag hungry. Caper wimpered and she wrapped her arms around him and stroked his forehead. Eventually, he slept.

She couldn't believe that Goff wouldn't come back. Not if he was able.

She lay in the sleeping bag, watching the gray dawn slide across the windows, and thought of all of the reasons why Goff might not have returned. He might have been arrested. A clerk in a store or a plainclothes cop might have caught him stuffing a package of hot dogs into his ripped coat lining. He could have been picked up when trying to snatch another old lady's purse. He thought that he was so smart. He wouldn't listen to her. He had probably tried something stupid and had been caught. He could be in jail, right now—or juvie, or whatever they called it where they threw fourteen-year olds.

But what if he had been hurt? Some hoods might've beat him up, just for laughs. He might have been hit by a car or a truck and be lying in a hospital ward, or in the morgue, waiting for somebody to identify him. Only nobody would ever show up. He'd lie there, unknown and unclaimed, and would eventually be deposited in an unmarked pauper's grave.

She hoped he wasn't dead. Just thinking about it made her want to scream. She needed him. Caper needed him. It was a dirty rotten trick for Goff to do this to them.

He smelled and he had a goofy sense of humor, but she liked him. She cared about him. She wanted him to return to them.

Had he gotten angry with them? Maybe that was it. Maybe he had decided to hell with her and Caper. She couldn't blame him if he had. They were nothing to him. Why should he risk his skin for them?

The more she thought about it, the more she believed that Goff had decided to live on his own again. He needed his independence. She and Caper would have to learn to survive alone.

The next morning, Caper stopped playing with the puppy. He sat down on the sleeping bag, cradling it against his chest. T.C. knew what was wrong. He was hungry.

He didn't protest, he didn't complain. He had been hungry before; he knew that he could do nothing about it. If somebody gave him food, he ate it; if not, he had to endure the hunger pangs. It was his acceptance that cut most deeply at T.C. He was used to being badly treated. In his life, it had been more the rule than the exception. He probably thought that she could feed him, but had, for some unknown reason, decided not to. Maybe he even believed that she was punishing him.

"What am I going to do with you?" He looked up at her, hugging the brown and gray pup to his cheek and stroking it with his hand.

"I should've known things couldn't go on the way they were. I should've known it was too good to last."

All morning, she waited for Goff to show up. Then she went out alone. She walked to a supermarket many blocks away, strolled up and down its aisles, and returned home with a package of hot dogs and an apple turnover inside her shirt.

All the way from the store back to the warehouse she expected to be arrested. It seemed amazing to her that every person in the store didn't know that she had stolen those hot dogs and that Hostess turnover.

They ate the hot dogs cold. Caper shared his with the puppy. T.C. let him have the entire apple turnover.

Would she get used to stealing? How many times would it take before she could be as casual about it as Goff? Did she *want* to become an expert shoplifter?

What other choice did she have?

That night, she watched Caper and his pet crawl into the sleeping bag. The pup slithered and struggled beneath the lumpy cover. Finally, it settled down and Caper dozed off. Later, the pup dug out from under the thick down padding and wandered around the room sniffing for food.

Afraid that it would awaken Caper, T.C. scooped it up and stroked its smooth, pointed head. It trembled in her hands, staring up at her expectantly, its skinny tail beating against her wrist.

"Tomorrow," she whispered. "Tomorrow, I'll get plenty of food for all of us."

Mid-morning, T.C. left Caper and the scratching, flea-chomping puppy and set off across town. She would find a supermarket where she had never been, a busy one where they wouldn't notice a twelve-year-old girl with crime in her heart. She stopped in a gas station restroom and scrubbed her face with cold water and gritty pink soap from a wall container and combed her hair with the remains of her pocket comb. She took a soggy paper towel to her tennis shoes, but it didn't help much.

She strode from sun to shadow, from shadow to sun, up and down the hills of San Francisco. One minute the November sun glared hot and white off the gray pavement, the next moment she plunged into the cool darkness angled across the street by a sun-blocking building.

Eventually, she came to half a dozen stores crowded around a cramped parking lot; it was nothing like the vast suburban shopping centers she had visited with her mother and father. In San Francisco land was too expensive to waste on sprawling parking lots and shopping centers. Paper banners announcing the week's specials hung over the plate-glass windows of the ugly pink supermarket. Wire shopping carts cluttered the entrance. Fear rose like vomit from T.C.'s stomach to her mouth, but she pushed her way through the revolving gate into the air-conditioned market.

Gaudy signs revolved on little platforms and arched over the aisles from the curved, airplane-hangerlike ceilings. The inside of the supermarket was like a carnival. Muzak droned through the artificially frigid air. Everything was bright, colorful, overwhelmingly cheerful. T.C. had never realized before how awful supermarkets were.

"Hey, what do you think you're doing?"

T.C. whirled around, but the voice wasn't aimed at her. A young mother was shouting at her kid, ordering him to put back a package of cheese-flavored nibbles that looked like paralyzed worms. The little boy whined, the dough-skinned woman screeched, finally dragging the kid by the arm as she charged down the aisle, using her shopping cart like a military vehicle. The only men in the store were the checkout clerks behind their cash registers and the butchers safe behind the high, glass-shielded meat counter.

Potato chips, corn chips, taco chips, tortilla chips: None of them tempted T.C. This time she would be sensible, taking only nourishing food. A can of tuna fish found its way into her jacket pocket, soon followed by a package of thin-sliced turkey meat. Okay, that took care of protein. What next? A couple of small cans of apple juice fit into the other pocket. It wasn't difficult to slide two Dolly Madison apple turnovers under her T-shirt. A few plums and several small apples found convenient hiding places inside her clothes. A couple of candy bars and a package of Lifesavers didn't cause any unsightly bulges in the back pockets of her jeans. After maneuvering a small bottle of vitamin pills into her jacket, she decided that she shouldn't push her luck.

She had reached the electric eye-activated glass doors when she realized that she didn't have any dog food. If she didn't bring home something for the puppy, Caper would feed it his own food, so she backtracked to the pet food aisle. Anxious to be out of the store, she snatched a couple of small cans from a shelf and jammed them under her jacket. When she turned to make her exit, she saw two men in green smocks watching her.

"Oh, hell."

For an instant, she considered trying to make a run for it, but she saw that she would never get away. Clerks suddenly crouched by all of the exits, and a uniformed policeman strode up the main aisle toward the pet food section. She was trapped, between Little Friskies and Purina Dog Chow.

Sure, she was guilty. But was it necessary for them to be so sarcastic? Was it necessary for them to make cute remarks as they watched her take the cans and packages out of her jacket and shirt? Why did the cop have to keep asking her if she knew that she was breaking the law when she took all those things? Of course she knew. Did they think she was retarded?

"Why?" they asked her. "Why did you do it?"

She shrugged her shoulders, studied a worn spot on the green composition tile floor. "I was hungry."

"Don't your parents feed you?"

"I don't live at home."

"Speak up, kid. I can't hear you."

"I said I don't live with my parents!"

She wouldn't tell them about Caper. Whatever happened, she wouldn't let them find out about Caper.

"You were hungry, huh?"

This was the policeman: tall, potbellied, small-eyed, sarcastic.

She answered his question with a nod.

"I guess you like horsemeat better than ordinary hamburger, huh?" He held the can of dog food close to her face. "It can't be the price, since you weren't paying for it, anyway."

She nodded again, vigorously. "Yeah. I love it. You oughta try it, sometime."

The cop glared at her. "Don't get smart with me, kid."

"I'm not being smart. I answered your dumb question."

"You're in serious trouble already, so you'd better watch it."

The merchandise, including both cans of dog food, was returned to the store and the cop led T.C. away. Housewives in bulging shorts and shiny acrylic wigs clutched their small offspring and stared at the young criminal. Old women gripped their grocery carts with palsied hands and shook their tightly curled heads. The younger generation, no respect for right and wrong, no fear of God: T.C. could read it on their faces.

She wanted to stick out her tongue, and would have if she hadn't suspected that the cop would smack her if she tried it.

Pedestrians stopped on the sidewalk and stared blatantly as the cop led her to his car. Her mask of defiance was slipping. Fear knotted her stomach. Kids pointed and an old man leaning on an aluminum crutch told the young black nurse holding his arm that delinquents like that girl oughta be whipped until they can't sit down.

"Sit in there and shut up!" ordered the policeman, shoving her into the back seat of his sedan.

A steel grille separated the rear of the car from the front. T.C. guessed that it was to prevent her from bopping the cop on his bald head. After all, she was a dangerous criminal. They had to watch out for her. She was capable of anything.

Sitting in that big car, staring through the steel mesh at the back of the cop's closely cropped neck as they drove through San Francisco, all T.C. could think of was Caper alone with his puppy in the warehouse. She could see that skinny kid huddled in the corner, waiting for her to return, watching the shadows fill the little room until he was completely in the dark. Would he try to light the candles that Goff had stolen? If he did, would he set himself or the warehouse on fire?

They weren't going to let her off with a warning. They'd be damned if they'd set her free. They'd keep at her until she told them where she lived, and then they'd send her back to Berkeley. That or juvenile hall. She had no choice: If she didn't tell them about Caper he'd die. He'd sit in that warehouse and die.

She had to admit that she hadn't done a very good job of taking care of that boy. She was a failure. She had tried to survive on her own in an adult world and she had made a mess of it, start to finish.

The next thing she knew, she was crying. At least, tears were sliding down her cheeks. She couldn't see a thing. She wasn't making any noise, but it was crying all the same.

I don't care, she told herself. Whatever they do to me, it doesn't matter. She had visions of them chaining her to a wall and taking a whip to her. But she knew that they wouldn't touch her. She was a child. That was her excuse and her protection, whether she had failed so badly. They couldn't make her feel worse than she already did. They might think that they had made her cry, but they were wrong. They would never understand what the tears represented—that there was no hope if you're a kid. You have to give up and wait out the sentence. You have to serve your time, like a criminal, and they can do what they want with you until the day when you become one of them. One of the free ones. A grown-up.

She had it all worked out, now. But it was too late. Goff had been wrong. It wasn't a matter of street smarts. It was simply understanding the true relationship between kids and adults.

The car stopped and she wiped her face on her sleeve and waited to be told what to do next.

11

How many days and nights had passed since she was picked up, since they had gone to fetch Caper at the warehouse? She had lost track.

The San Francisco police hadn't bullied her. She couldn't accuse them of bullying her. She had been surprised by how much they had understood of her situation. A runaway. Yeah, they had seen that and had believed her when she said that she was taking food only because she needed it. The one in charge at the station had told her that he could see that she wasn't a thief. All he wanted to do was send her home to her parents. There was no question of jail or reform school. He believed that children should be with their mothers and fathers. In his opinion, she had suffered enough.

He was a nice middle-aged man, with a white crew cut bristling on his head and blue eyes that seemed to see right into her brain. She wondered if this tough old cop could read her thoughts as they passed under her forehead. She felt certain that he suspected something about Caper, the way he kept asking her where she'd been living.

When she told him that she stayed one night with a strange man she met in the Hot Dog Palace, he shook his head, lowered his voice, and brought his face within inches of hers and asked if she knew how dangerous that was? Deliberately, to shock him, she told him that she had slept several nights in the excavations below Mission Street. He shook his head again and looked very serious.

"How did you live?" he asked her. "How did you get food?"

"I bought it," she told him, with the patience of an adult talking to a feebleminded child. "I had money. Until it was stolen."

"*Then* what did you do?" He smiled understandingly: "Somebody stole your money, so you stole food? Is that it?"

She nodded. What else could she do?

But he kept on questioning her. His eyes sparkled with suspicion. He knew that she was hiding something—or somebody.

She knew that she had to tell about Caper and the puppy. Otherwise nobody would know to take care of them. But she wanted to think about it first, and figure out the best way to do it. The cop kept after her, sneaking up on her, asking trick questions, trying to catch her off guard.

He liked kids. Didn't he keep telling her that he liked kids? He had a couple of granddaughters, himself, he told her, and he knew how girls her age felt. He didn't know, of course, but she didn't contradict him. He was trying to be nice. She had to give him credit for that.

"San Francisco isn't a safe place for a young girl to wander around alone, young lady. Are you aware of that? There are men who take advantage of young girls. Use them to sell drugs—or their bodies. Yes, even as young as you. How old are you? Thirteen, fourteen?"

"Twelve."

"Even twelve-year-olds. These people have no decency. They don't care about anything but getting what they want out of you. Don't smile. I'm not joking."

But she was smiling from embarrassment, not humor. She wished that he would end his sermon and do whatever he intended to do with her.

"You can't even trust women." He looked particularly satisfied with that remark, as if he had headed off a dangerous conclusion that he had spied lurking in T.C.'s brain. "Sometimes, these bad men have women working for them who pick up unsuspecting girls like you, runaways with nobody to take care of them, and gain their confidence. One thing leads to another and before the girls know it, they're trapped."

"Nothing like that happened to me!"

"It could have. That's the point. You were lucky."

She nodded. Perhaps she had been lucky. But she didn't feel lucky.

"You must be worried about whoever you were with?"

"What do you mean?"

"You know—your fellow runaways. You weren't alone. I know that."

"How . . .?"

She stopped herself. She mustn't admit anything. Make them work for each fact. They were adults. She had to remember that they couldn't be trusted. Not even this joker with his crew cut and his grandfather act. Adults say one thing and do something else. Maybe they can't help it. Maybe that's what being a grown-up does to you. But she wasn't going to trust them.

"We'll probably find out that they were picked up, too."

He looked directly at her, trying to read her face. He didn't know as much as he was pretending to know.

She responded with an offhand gesture, and waited to see what would happen next.

"How do you know they're still alive? I explained to you, T.C., things happen in this city. The Tenderloin isn't a playground. We're talking about pimps and prostitutes, dope fiends. Criminals, T.C. Ex-convicts. Murderers, even. This is for real. It's not a game."

She covered her ears with her hands. "I didn't say it was a game!"

He had done it again. Had made her cry. Damn him.

"Okay," she murmured, wiping her nose with a tissue that he passed across the desk to her. "I guess I have to tell you. He needs somebody to look after him. He's just a little kid. His name is Caper. He's only about nine years old. Maybe eight. He can't talk. That's why we ran away together: because his parents beat up on him. You know, abused him, like in that TV show. They burned him with cigarettes and knocked him around. Tied him up, sometimes, and wouldn't let him go to the bathroom. Didn't even feed him. They were going to kill him. And that's the truth. What I'm saying isn't any game, either!"

In spite of himself, the police captain looked impressed by that outpouring of words and emotion.

"I stole him. I snuck into his house and took him with me. There was no place to hide him at my place, not where they wouldn't find him and send him back. And then he'd get beat up worse. It was his mother, his own mother! And his stepfather. They hate him, or something. I couldn't let him stay there. I took fifty dollars from Neil and we came to San Francisco. I thought fifty bucks would last a long time, but a guy we met stole most of it. He had a beard like Neil's. That's why I trusted him. I was so damned stupid. He ran off with thirty dollars! We would've starved, but Goff helped us. He was the one person we met who didn't try to rob us. He's a kid, too. That's why. But he went away and didn't come back. I don't know where. So I had to steal, because Caper and the puppy were hungry. The store people caught me when I went back for the dog food. If it hadn't been for that dog food, nobody ever would've known. Now you've got me and I guess you're gonna send me home. I don't care. But I'm worried about Caper. You've got to promise not to send him back to his mother and stepfather, before I'll tell you where he is. 'Cause they'll *kill* him."

Exhausted, emotionally drained, T.C. quivered like a young tree in a storm. The captain came around his desk and pushed a chair under her. She collapsed into it, holding her head in her hands. She couldn't stop trembling.

"Don't worry, T.C. If what you say is true, about the boy's parents, we won't make him go back to them. We don't like to see children mistreated, either."

"Okay," she said, at last. "I'll tell you where he is, but that's all. I'm not going to tell you where he used to live. Send somebody nice out to get him, somebody who won't scare him too much. Or, better yet, can I go, too? Please? So he won't be afraid? He's used to me. Grown-ups scare him."

She glared at the police captain as if accusing him of belonging to that terrible race of giant beings. He nodded, and said that he understood. When he announced that she could go in the squad car to pick up her friend, she realized, to her surprise, that he *did* understand.

"And the puppy!" she reminded him. "Don't forget the puppy!"

"And the puppy."

A pair of young policemen were sent with T.C. to the warehouse. The two-tone squad car drove up and down the hills and between dark buildings, while T.C. pressed her face to the window and tried to figure out which gloomy street was the right one. The cop with the acne scars all over his forehead, cheeks, and neck asked her if she was trying to give them the runaround, but then she recognized the alley and the warehouse with the broken ". . . HNSON BROS." sign.

"Over there. The door is around the corner."

The cops hesitated in front of the warehouse, staring up at the stark, weathered facade.

"There? You were living in *there*? Jesus."

T.C. pushed open the door and stepped over the high threshold. The huge empty darkness flooded around her (it seemed years, not hours since she had seen Caper), but she made herself be tough. It was a matter of honor that she reveal no emotion to the two cops.

They waded through the gray light, shoeleather on floorboards the only sound in the vast building. Then, as they climbed the swaying, groaning old stairs, a wail rose out of the walls, echoing in the giant cavern of the warehouse. It grew louder and louder, an animal cry of hunger and despair. The dog. The poor starving pup, trapped with Caper in the room upstairs.

She started to run, but the cop clamped his hand down on her shoulder. He thought that she was trying to get away.

She shook her head and pointed to the row of cubicles on the mezzanine. He nodded, and they stealthily approached the door that she indicated. The police acted as if they expected to find a bank robber holed up in that tiny office, instead of a skinny kid and a starving puppy.

One of the cops pushed the door open, peered inside. Then he nodded that T.C. could go on in.

"Caper!"

He wasn't there. The puppy leaped at her, licking her hand, whining and barking, begging to be fed. The place stunk of dog mess and filth; the pup had turned things upside down, trying to find a scrap to eat. The sleeping bag had been chewed and clawed until it was little more than rags and scattered stuffing.

T.C. darted from one side of the small room to the other, throwing aside the remains of the sleeping bag, the pile of clothes and rags in the corner, although she knew that Caper wasn't there.

"He's hiding! He heard us come in and got scared. He must be hiding in one of the other rooms."

"Maybe somebody took him away."

T.C.'s head jerked around and she glared at the cop who dared to suggest such a possibility. She wanted to smash in his smug, acne-scarred face. Instead, she violently shook her head and picked up the puppy.

"No! He's hiding. I know he is. He's scared and hiding."

She ran past the cop, onto the mezzanine, groping for the door to the next office. The pup licked at her face with his rough tongue.

"Caper! It's me. Caper, where are you?"

"I thought you said this kid was deaf and dumb?" The cop was right behind her.

"What? No. I never said that. I said he didn't talk. I didn't say he was deaf. I never said that."

She pushed open the first door, but the office was empty except for drifts of dust and an ancient calendar hanging cockeyed on the stained wall. The puppy whimpered and slobbered over her face.

"Caper! Please, where are you?"

Crashing into the wall, stumbling around the two policemen, she ran to the next office, pushed open the gray glass door, and tripped over an object cowering in the dark. The dog let out a howl and jumped from her arms, and she knelt in the dust beside the huddled creature that had caused her to fall.

"Caper . . ."

She lifted him up, held him to her, trying to make him look at her. His eyes were open, but unfocused. Dust and cobwebs exploded from him like seeds from a dandelion. She could smell that he had messed his pants again.

"Caper, it's me. I said I'd come back, didn't I?"

She wiped his face with her sleeve and hugged him to her, as if she believed that she could squeeze recognition into him.

"He's pretty far gone, if you ask me."

"No! He's scared. You shut up. You don't know a thing about it. He was afraid I'd run out on him, but now I'm back everything is going to be okay. Isn't it, Caper? Isn't it?"

She was almost screaming at him.

He stared at her, his mouth hanging open, then his hand fell against her shoulder. The dog leaped up on them, licking at first one and then the other, utttering little barks, smacking them with its tail.

Of course it was begging for food, but there was love in those sloppy, long-tongued licks, too. Love for her, love for Caper, love for Goff, wherever he was. All the love in the world existed in this funny-looking, long-tailed pup.

"We better go," said the one policeman, the taller, younger one, not the scarred one who made the remarks that infuriated T.C. "So we can clean him up and give him some food. And the dog, too."

He added the latter, as if in answer to T.C.'s change of expression, although that wasn't precisely what she had been thinking.

"We'll take good care of him, really."

T.C. nodded. She was resigned, now, to whatever happened.

"I suppose he's too weak to walk down to the car himself," said the acne-scarred cop. "Christ, he stinks!"

T.C. hated that cop and his acne-scarred face and neck, but as she stared at him, hating him with all of her might, she experienced a reaction completely new to her. She felt bad for hating his acne scars; she could hate him, that is, what he did to her, but his scars had done nothing to deserve her hatred. Neil would probably say that she was growing up, but she knew that it had nothing to do with becoming older. Maybe she was turning into a person, but that didn't mean a grown-up—not the way she visualized grown-ups.

The scarless, shorter cop carried Caper downstairs and out to the police sedan. He didn't say a word about Caper's smelly pants. T.C. transported the puppy.

Stepping from the darkness of the warehouse into the daylight nearly blinded her. Why, she wondered, did the sky have to be so painfully blue? At least, it could be a sympathetic gray. It was the kind of day her father pronounced "clear and cold" when he jumped astride his bicycle in the mornings. And "clear and cold" just about summed it up for her: Never had her misery been so clear or her body so cold.

She trembled all the way to the station, sometimes so violently that the dog in her arms whimpered.

A radio, turned low, but not low enough, played disco music between commercials. Adults in all sizes and shapes, like Heinz's Fifty-seven varieties, came and went with confusing rapidity. She was in the police station, face to face with Power.

T.C. switched from leaning on one foot to leaning on the other, as she listened to the captain talking first to Malvina and then to Neil and finally to T.C.'s mother. It was arranged that Neil would drive T.C.'s parents over to San Francisco to pick her up. The captain never did seem to understand that T.C. lived in a commune, but she saw no reason to explain it to him.

"What about Caper?" she asked the captain. "What's going to happen to him?"

"That depends on you, T.C."

"What do you mean?"

She felt that old suspicion of adults returning. His tone of voice, grandfather gruff but syrupy, too, told her that he was not to be trusted.

"Since he can't, or won't talk, you're going to have to tell us where he lives, aren't you?"

"But. . . ."

"His parents must be worried about him."

"Didn't you listen to me? I told you about his mother and his stepfather. They hate him. They tortured him. Can't you understand? They starved him and beat him and made him sit in his own mess! They burned him with cigarettes. For fun! I *saw* them do it! He still has marks on him. They're mostly better, but not all of them. You can see the scars. How do you think he got those marks on him?"

"Don't get excited, T.C. We all want to do what's best for the boy."

She hated it most when adults tried to sound reasonable. It meant that they were closing their ears to whatever you had to say and intended to bully you into doing things their way.

"I won't do it. I won't tell you where he . . . where his mother and that man live. They're probably not there anymore, anyway. They were going to move. They lived in that house like it was a motel. They didn't belong there. They were from someplace else."

She knew that she wasn't making sense, but she wouldn't let the police send Caper back to those two monsters.

"I don't care if you put me in jail, I'm not going to tell you."

The captain's false teeth showed in the middle of his pink face as he smiled down on her, rubbing the bristle of his white crew cut with one of his pink hands.

"Nobody's going to put you in jail, T.C. Don't worry."

She stuck out her jaw: "I'm not! I'm not worried, at all! Where . . . what will happen to him? I mean, if he's not going back to his mother and stepfather?"

"He'll become a ward of the state. A judge will have to decide his case. Probably, he'll be assigned to a foster home. If the court can find one that will take him. He's a special case. It might not be easy."

"He's a good kid! Really, he is. He's no trouble. He never does anything bad. If people are nice to him, he's just fine!"

"I'm sure he is, T.C. We'll see what we can work out. I promise, we'll take everything you said into consideration."

I'll bet you will, thought T.C. I'll just bet you will!

More than an hour dragged by while T.C. and Caper (one of the cops had taken him into the men's room and cleaned him up as best as he could) sat on wooden chairs in the outer office waiting for her parents to arrive.

A black woman police officer brought T.C. and Caper hamburgers and little cartons of milk with red and white striped plastic straws. They shared their milk and meat with the puppy. Later, the lady cop brought them paper cups of vanilla ice cream and little wooden spoons shaped like paddles to eat it with. She was trying to be nice, but it depressed T.C. How could anybody think that hamburgers and vanilla ice cream would make everything all right?

What if they take him away, T.C. thought, as she watched Caper sucking at the ice cream on his paddle, and put him in a foster home?

She might never see him again. They might not let her see him. They might think that she would make him run away again. How would she know what happened to him? Or if the people in the foster home were nice or mean, if they let him keep the puppy, if he was happy or not? She wouldn't know if he were ever able to talk more than those three words. He might forget her.

As she watched him dropping gobs of vanilla ice cream on the scuffed, age-darkened wood floor for the pup to lick, this thought hurt T.C. the most: She didn't want Caper to forget her.

The acne-scarred cop passed through the room, pausing in the doorway and surreptitiously rubbing some crust from the corner of one eye while staring at T.C. and Caper. He pretended that he was only rubbing the side of his nose, but he was digging at the crust in the corner of the eye and rubbing it all over the place before finally catching it under his nail and flicking it off, across the room.

Then T.C. heard voices and the sound of shoes running clumsily over the worn floors of the police station, and she knew that they must be here. She took a deep breath, as if she were about to dive into the deep end of a swimming pool, and faced the frosted glass panes of the big double doors across the room.

They fussed over her. Christ, how they fussed! But she let them paw at her and shout and weep and scold—there was plenty of that!—and kept her mind narrowed on one thing: Caper. Only by concentrating and putting all of her strength on Caper could she survive. They overwhelmed her with their combined apologies and scoldings, their explanations and accusations.

Now, here she was, back in Berkeley, on the same bed that she had slept in for years, but her heart was still in San Francisco with Caper and Goff. Her body was here, where the grown-ups had brought it, but the rest of her, the important part of her, was across the bay. Why else was she waking up every night with those dreams? Why couldn't she "adjust," as Neil and her father called it, to a "normal" routine again? Because she didn't want to adjust to a so-called normal life. She wanted to find out what they had done to Caper; she wanted to see him again and make sure that they weren't doublecrossing her.

Neil had admitted that he shouldn't have been so ready to say no when T.C. had begged him to adopt Caper. He agreed that he should have listened and should have taken the time to investigate the facts about the boy's parents. A lot of good his admissions did now.

Sitting crosslegged on her bed, beneath the torn "Don't Tread on Me!" flag, in the girls' bedroom on the top floor of the Berkeley house, stroking the brown and gray puppy, T.C. resolved that she would convince her parents that they had to assume responsibility for Caper. They believed in saving the whales and protecting the porpoises and they campaigned for the lettuce workers and the grape pickers and fought against the atomic power plants and nuclear bombs. Okay, then they could face up to the fact that Caper Scanlon was one more being that needed them, and the "moral" thing to do was to adopt him. Protect him.

She would keep after them until she wore them down, until they wore down the authorities.

It was like wheels in a machine, you had to keep them moving, one after the other, grinding away, until the end result was achieved. You couldn't ever let up, or the whole machine clanged to a halt.

She had hated on sight the man who took Caper away from the police station. His features had possessed a mushy quality, like the pink sponge that Malvina used to wash dishes. He hadn't cared about Caper or her or anybody else. First thing, he had announced that the dog had to be left behind. At least, T.C.'s parents and Neil had let her bring the pup home to Berkeley. But she would never forget that awful moment when that man had plucked the dog out of Caper's arms and thrust it at her. Caper had looked around helplessly, and then had shriveled back into himself, closing up like a sea anenomes when you poke a pencil into its middle. Then the man had dragged him away, because rules were rules.

T.C. apologized to Neil about the fifty dollars. She promised that she would pay it back, a little at a time. He told her that it didn't matter; he wasn't worried about the money. Only two things were important, he said: that she had run away and that she was coming home.

"We want you to come home," he told her. "All of us. You're part of our family. We need you."

Need. What does that mean? Caper needs her. She needs Goff. They all need each other. Yet the grown-ups wouldn't let them be together. The grown-ups' needs always come first.

She sat up in the bed, stroking the pup on the top of the head, letting him lick her face with his rough tongue, and concentrated on Caper. Maybe, if she concentrated hard enough, he would think of her, too. Maybe, somehow, it would bring them back together.

T.C. was surprised, as the days passed and Thanksgiving came and went and Christmas decorations crowded store windows, that her strongest ally was Neil. Her parents didn't understand her feelings about Caper, but Neil seemed almost as eager as she was, now, to have the boy in the commune. Maybe he liked the idea of rescuing Caper. He had always thought of the commune as an "island of sanity" in a crazy, cruel world. Whatever it was, Neil listened to T.C.'s descriptions of Caper's past existence and agreed to do everything that he could to convince the court and the social workers and anybody else who needed convincing that they would give Caper a good and stable home.

During the day, she went to school and did her homework, trying to catch up with her classes, and wandered around Berkeley, as she had before. One afternoon, she walked past the duplex where Caper had lived. It looked deserted, but she didn't hang around long enough to be certain. Neil had explained to her that if the court demanded her to give this address she would have to comply or be held in contempt, which meant that she would be in awful trouble. She didn't quite understand what that meant, but she was relieved to see that no lights were visible in the windows, that crumpled advertising fliers lay on the doorsteps and a yellowed newspaper was half-hidden in the weeds.

At home, sometimes, when she walked into the kitchen or passed the library or wandered into the bedroom, people stopped talking, and she knew that they had been discussing her. It didn't bother her as much as she had thought it would. The kids wanted to hear stories of her adventures, but she didn't feel like recounting the saga of her days as a runaway. The parts that were important to her were too private to share, and the rest she wanted to forget.

She felt as if she had grown up beyond her twelve years during those days in San Francisco. She had experienced things that other kids her own age couldn't even guess about. She wasn't a kid anymore, but she wasn't an adult, either. Caught between childhood and maturity, she was more confused than ever, but she learned that she was tougher than she had suspected.

Without intending to, T.C. kept to herself, spending hours walking or sitting alone and thinking. There was so much to think about. She looked at the world with new eyes. She seemed to be able to see through people. No longer did she feel hostile toward adults. She realized that they were only people, too. Life wasn't easy for anybody. You did the best you could, and hoped things would work out. Maybe she was no wiser than she had been before she ran away, but perhaps she was a little more tolerant.

The others asked questions because they were curious, but she knew that even if she gave them answers, even if they listened to the answers—which they probably wouldn't— they wouldn't understand, so she avoided the people and the problems of questions and answers. The question that she cared most about was the one of Caper, and she had to wait for the people in authority to decide what the answer would be.

Other questions about her future worried her, too. "What about Oregon?" she asked her father.

"What about it?"

"Are we . . . is the commune moving up there? What's happening?"

"I thought you knew. Sure, we're all going up there next summer. We're going to fix up the farmhouse and construct a new dormitory and another building that'll be a recreation hall and meeting place. Neil has all kinds of plans. It's very exciting. He showed home movies of the farm when . . . while you were away. It's a beautiful place. You'll love it, T.C. And there's a good high school nearby, I've heard. We'll be happy in Oregon, T.C."

T.C. nodded and wandered out to the garage. But when she looked into the storeroom, she was startled to find it empty. Somebody had cleaned it out. The old sofa, the ancient tools, the cupboards of mason jars, the decades of garbage: Everything was gone. Just the bare grease-stained concrete floor and the weathered wooden walls remained.

Already, they're preparing to move, she thought.

Soon, they would have one foot in this existence, in California, and one foot in the new life waiting for them in Oregon. They would expect her to share their enthusiasm. Maybe life up there wouldn't be so bad. Caper might like the farm. He had probably never seen a real cow or a goat or a pig. And he could run free in the fields, as he had that day on the beach, and get healthy and strong again. The puppy would like the farm, too.

She could see Caper and the dog, full-grown, running up a dirt road, past an old barn, and hear him calling to her, shouting her name.

She wanted to believe that the picture would come true.